JOHANN DAVID WYSS'S

THE SWISS FAMILY
ROBINSON

A GRAPHIC NOVEL
BY MARTIN POWELL &
GERARDO SANDOVAL

STONE ARCH BOOKS
A CAPSTONE IMPRINT

Graphic Revolve is published by Stone Arch Books
A Capstone Imprint
1710 Roe Crest Drive, North Mankato, Minnesota 56003
www.capstonepub.com

Cataloging-in-Publication Data is available at the Library
of Congress website.
Hardcover ISBN: 978-1-4965-0017-5
Paperback ISBN: 978-1-4965-0036-6

Summary: A family from Switzerland is shipwrecked
on a deserted island. They discover that the island is
filled with plants and animals they've never seen before.
Unfortunately, not all of the creatures are friendly.

Common Core back matter written by Dr. Katie Monnin.

Color by Benny Fuentes.

Designer: Bob Lentz
Assistant Designer: Peggie Carley
Editor: Donald Lemke
Assistant Editor: Sean Tulien
Creative Director: Heather Kindseth
Editorial Director: Michael Dahl
Publisher: Ashley C. Andersen Zantop

Printed in the United States of America.
122018   000059

TABLE OF CONTENTS

ABOUT CASTAWAYS AND DESERTED ISLANDS..5
CAST OF CHARACTERS..6

CHAPTER 1
SHIPWRECKED!..8

CHAPTER 2
BUILDING A NEW HOME..24

CHAPTER 3
A DEADLY MYSTERY..36

CHAPTER 4
ISLAND OF GOOD FORTUNE..44

CHAPTER 5
FRITZ'S DISCOVERY..49

CHAPTER 6
THE CAVE CREATURE..55

CHAPTER 7
RESCUED FROM PARADISE..61

ABOUT THE RETELLING AUTHOR AND ILLUSTRATOR....................................66
GLOSSARY..67
COMMON CORE ALIGNED READING AND WRITING QUESTIONS...................68

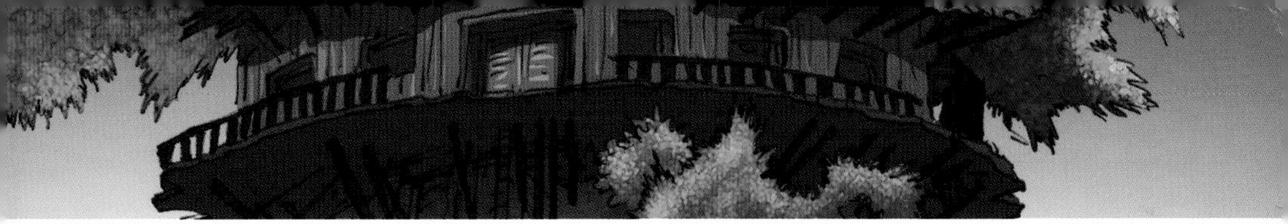

ABOUT CASTAWAYS AND DESERTED ISLANDS

Many movies, television shows, and books tell stories about people stranded on deserted islands. But could someone really get lost at sea and survive like the family in *The Swiss Family Robinson*?

Even with more than 6 billion people in the world, finding a place to get stranded isn't that difficult. Thousands of islands have no people living on them at all. In fact, the country of Indonesia has more than 6,000 uninhabited islands.

The largest uninhabited island in the world isn't small at all. Devon Island in Canada is an impressive 21,231 square miles. That's nearly as big as West Virginia!

So, finding a place to get lost is easy . . . but how long could a human survive without food or water? Surprisingly, humans can last nearly a month without any food. In fact, magician David Blaine lasted an incredible 44 days without eating in 2003. Finding water is much more important, though. Experts say that more than three days without water can be lethal.

If you are stranded on a deserted island, look for coconuts. These nuts are an excellent source of both food and hydration. The husks can be used to make rope, and coconut oil can help repel pesky insects such as mosquitoes.

So, surviving on a deserted island is possible (at least for a while), but has anyone ever done it? Many people have lasted a few days after a shipwreck or a plane crash, but only a few can be called real-life castaways. Perhaps the most famous castaway was a Scottish sailor named Alexander Selkirk. In September 1704, Selkirk was left stranded on a small island off the coast of Chile. With only a few tools and a musket, Selkirk survived alone for four years and four months. After he was rescued in February 1709, Selkirk wrote a book about his experience. A few years later, author Daniel Defoe turned Selkirk's story into a novel called *Robinson Crusoe*. This book has inspired many other adventure stories, including *The Swiss Family Robinson*.

Another famous castaway, Tom Neale, wasn't exactly stranded on a deserted island, but he did choose to live there! In 1952, Neale settled on a small island in the Pacific Ocean called Suwarrow. With only a few supplies, he lived by himself on the island for 15 of the next 25 years. He grew small gardens, raised chickens, caught fish, and ate coconuts. Shortly after his death in 1977, the island was declared a National Heritage Park. A small memorial on the island bears an inscription that reads, "Tom Neale lived his dream on this island."

CAST OF CHARACTERS

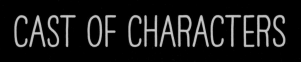

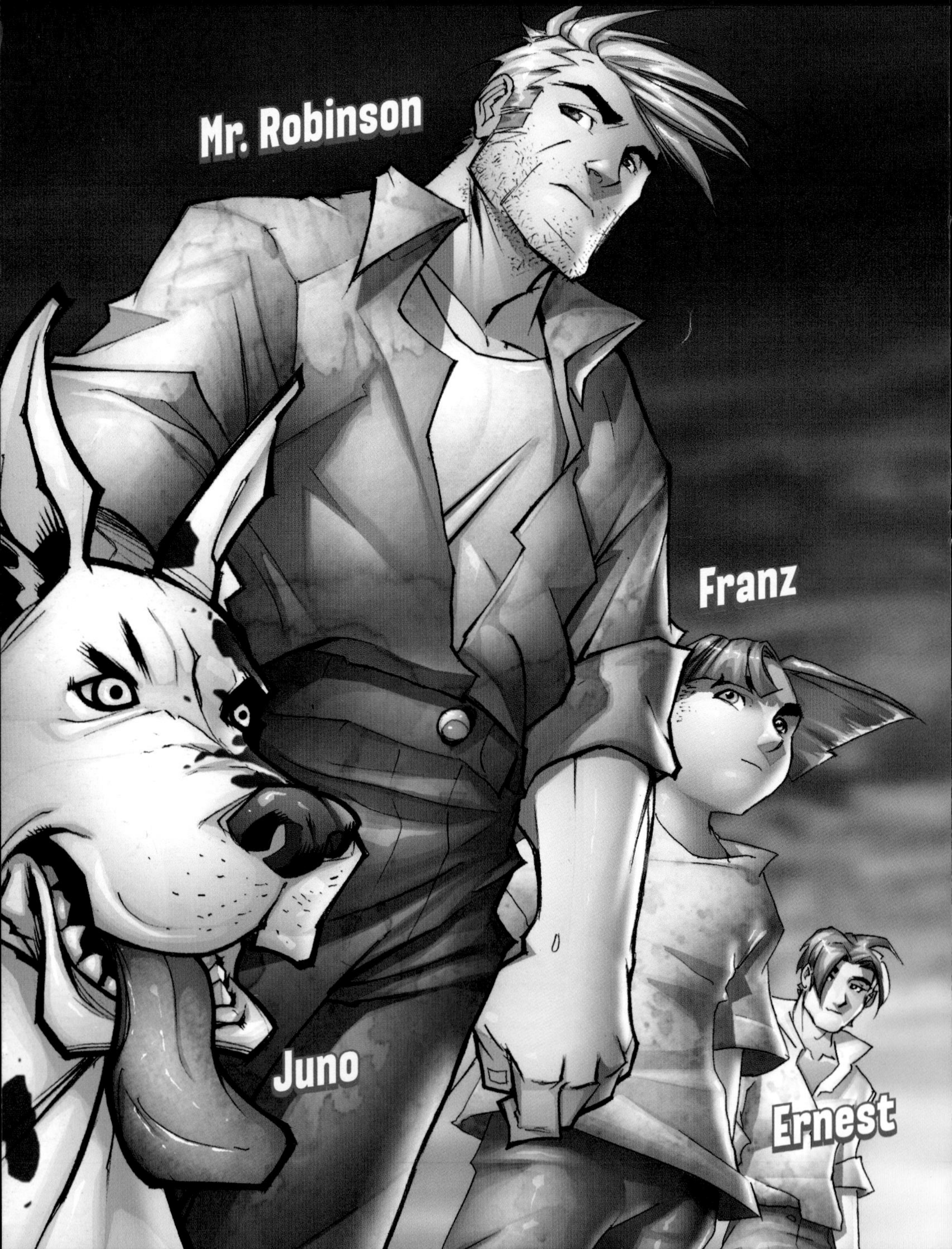
Mr. Robinson
Franz
Juno
Ernest

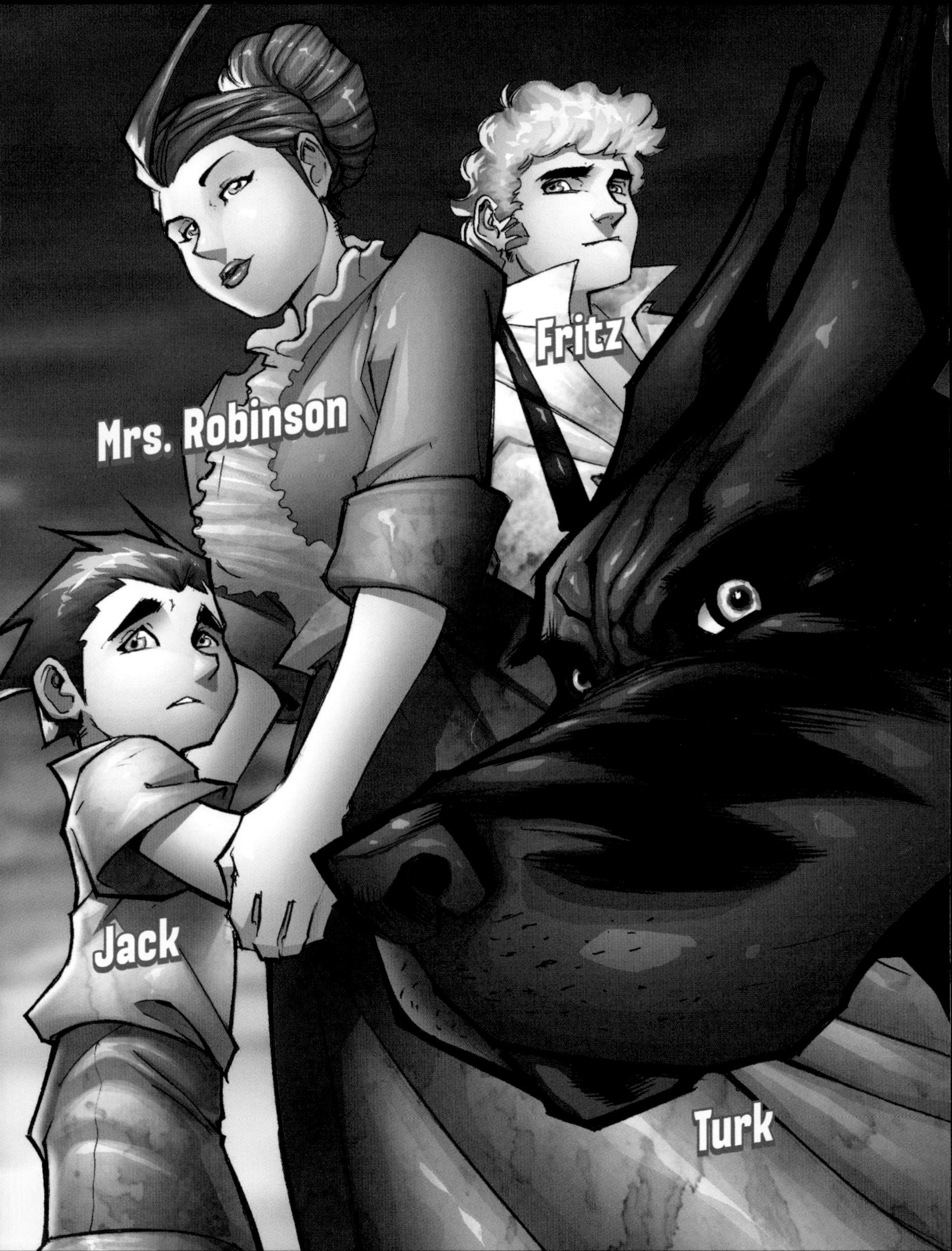
Mrs. Robinson
Fritz
Jack
Turk

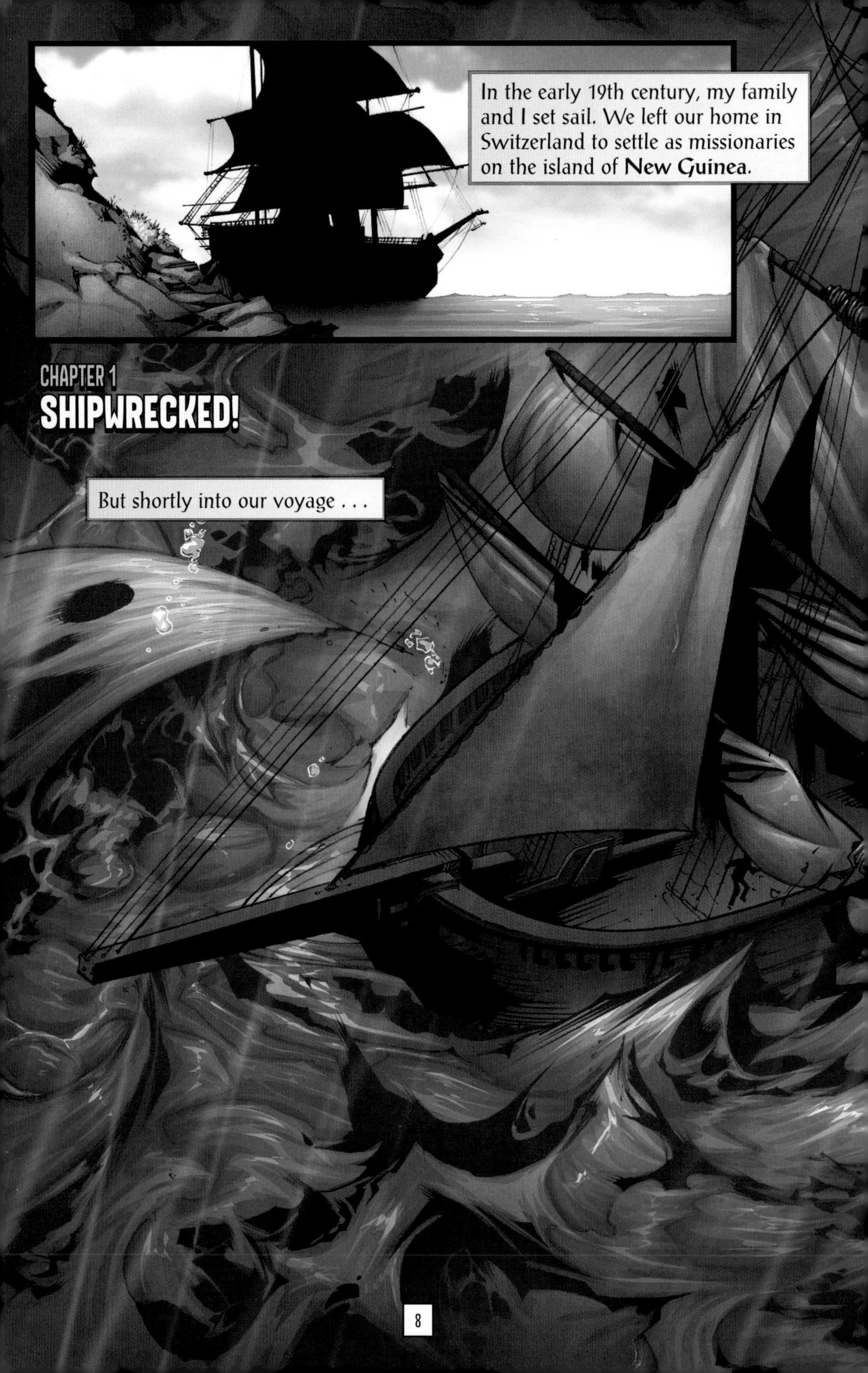
In the early 19th century, my family and I set sail. We left our home in Switzerland to settle as missionaries on the island of New Guinea.
CHAPTER 1
SHIPWRECKED!
But shortly into our voyage . . .

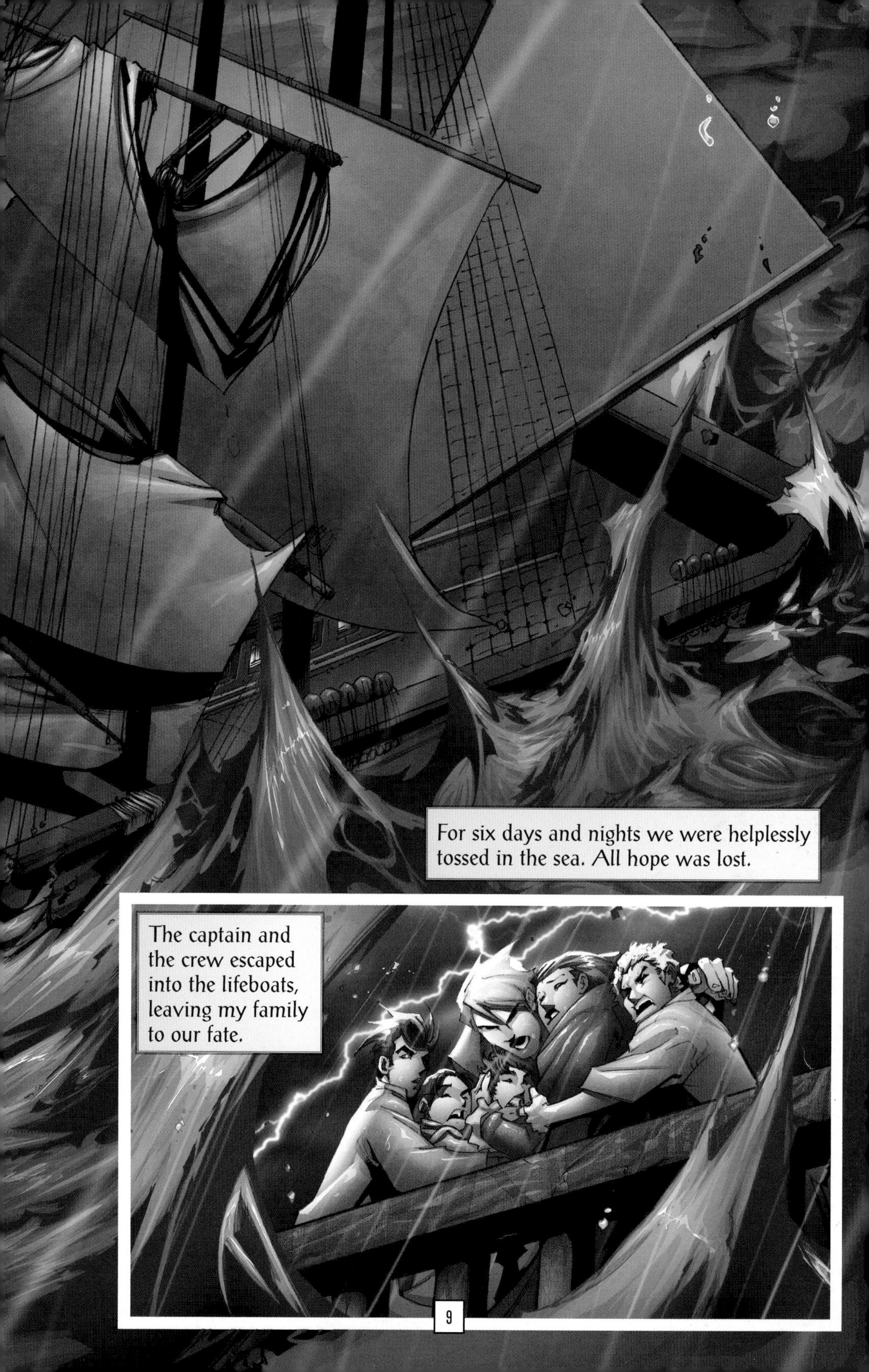
For six days and nights we were helplessly tossed in the sea. All hope was lost.
The captain and the crew escaped into the lifeboats, leaving my family to our fate.

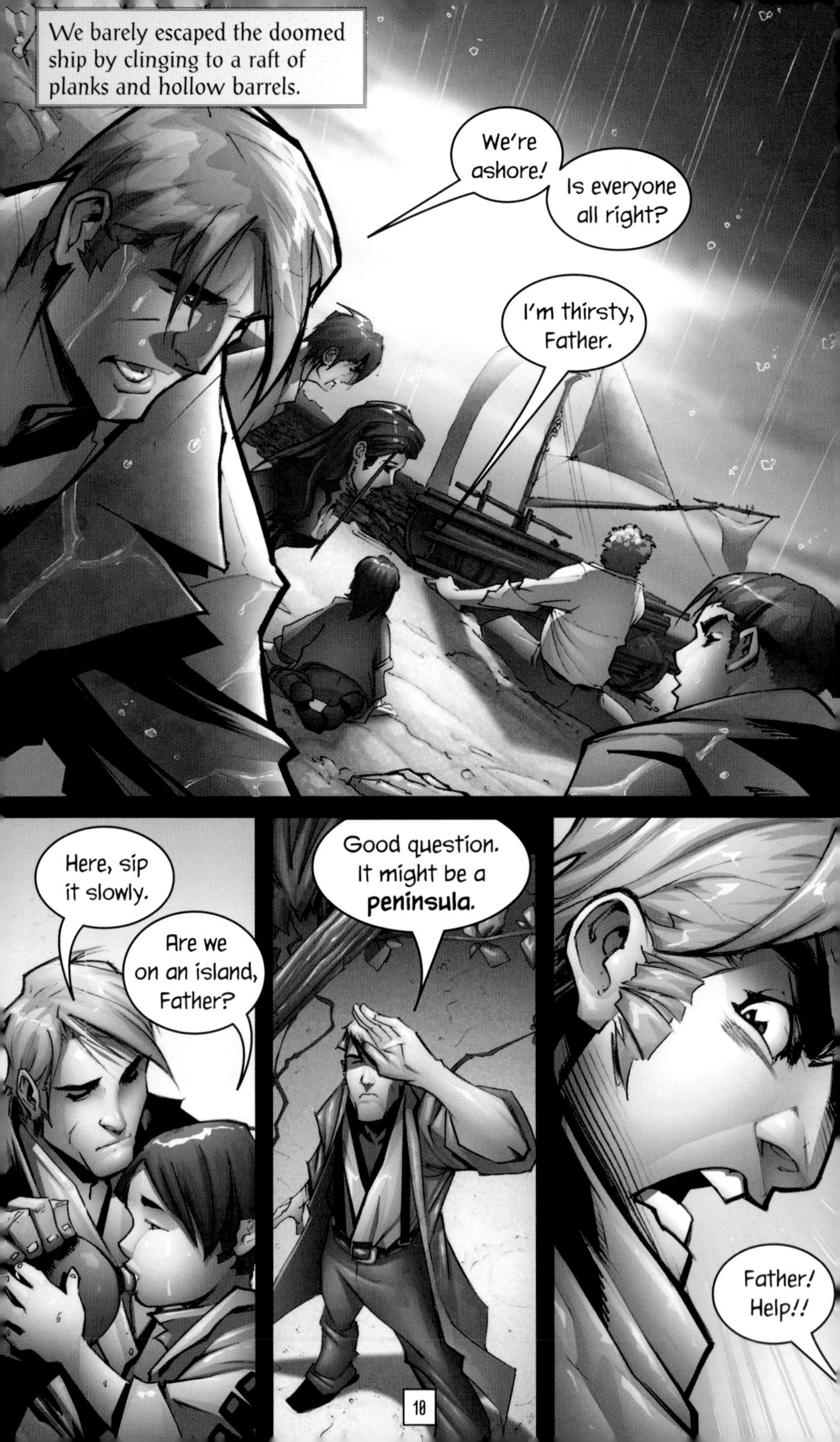
We barely escaped the doomed ship by clinging to a raft of planks and hollow barrels.
We're ashore!
Is everyone all right?
I'm thirsty, Father.
Here, sip it slowly.
Are we on an island, Father?
Good question. It might be a **peninsula.**
Father! Help!!

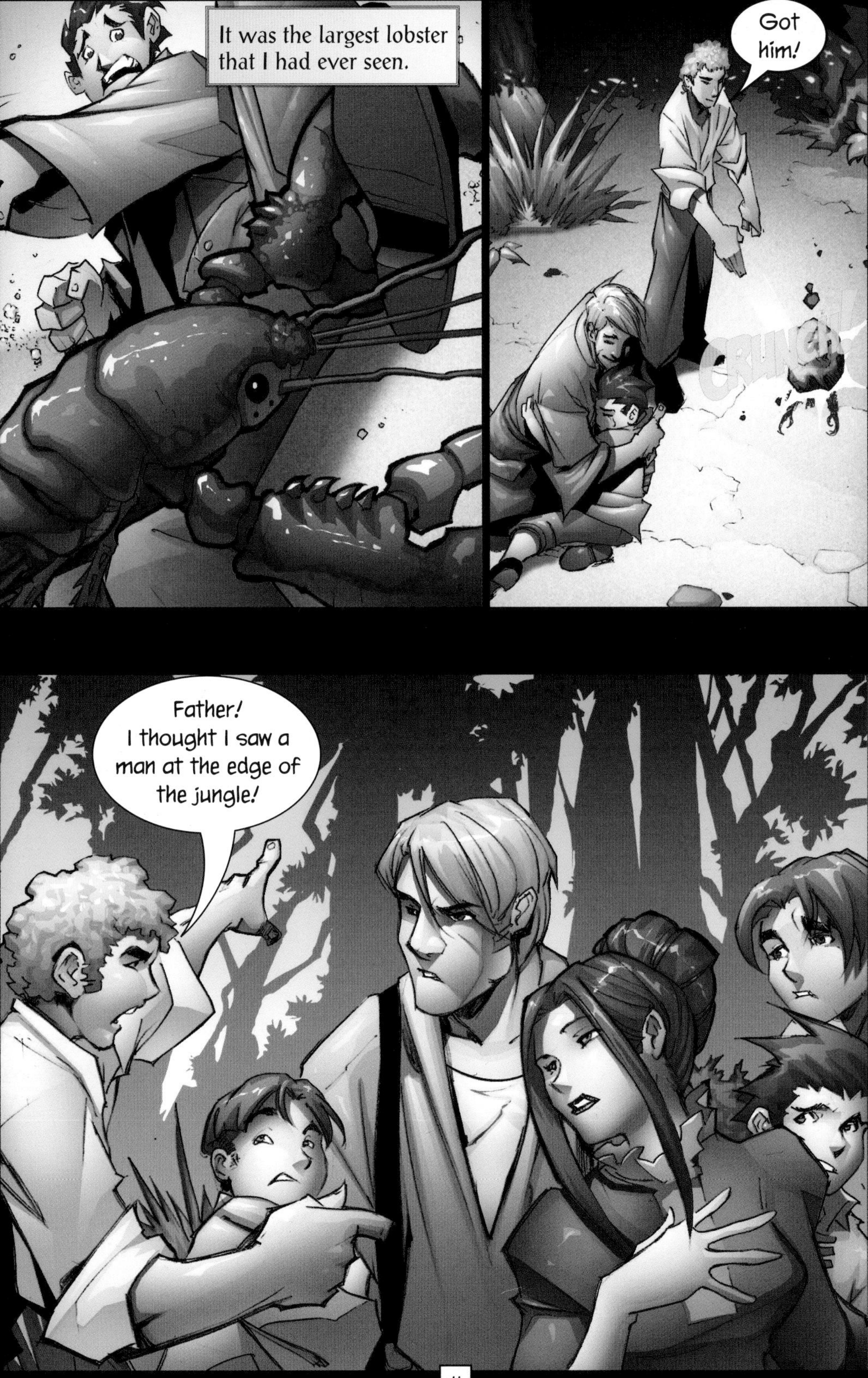
It was the largest lobster that I had ever seen.
Got him!
Father! I thought I saw a man at the edge of the jungle!

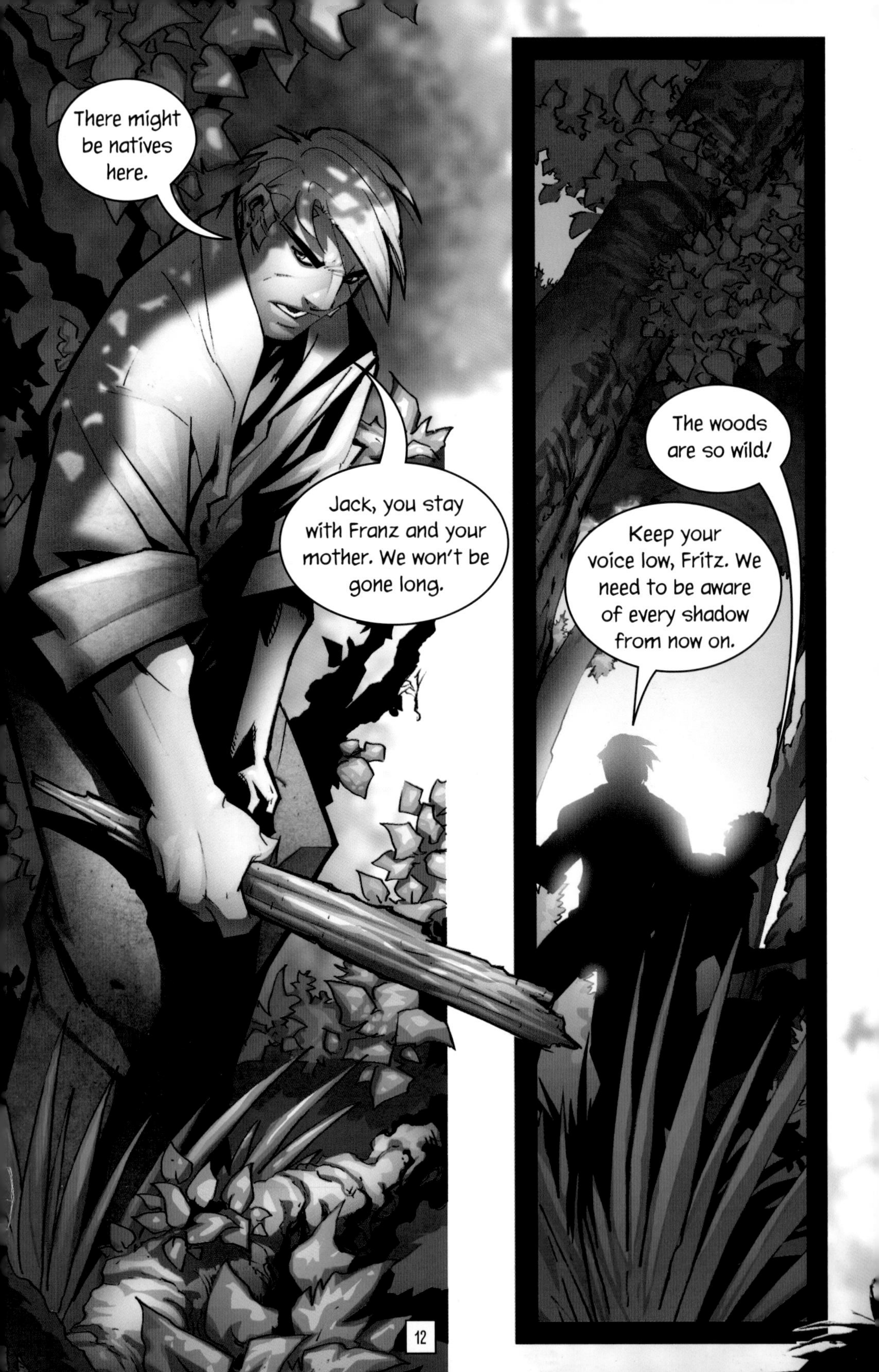
There might be natives here.
Jack, you stay with Franz and your mother. We won't be gone long.
The woods are so wild!
Keep your voice low, Fritz. We need to be aware of every shadow from now on.

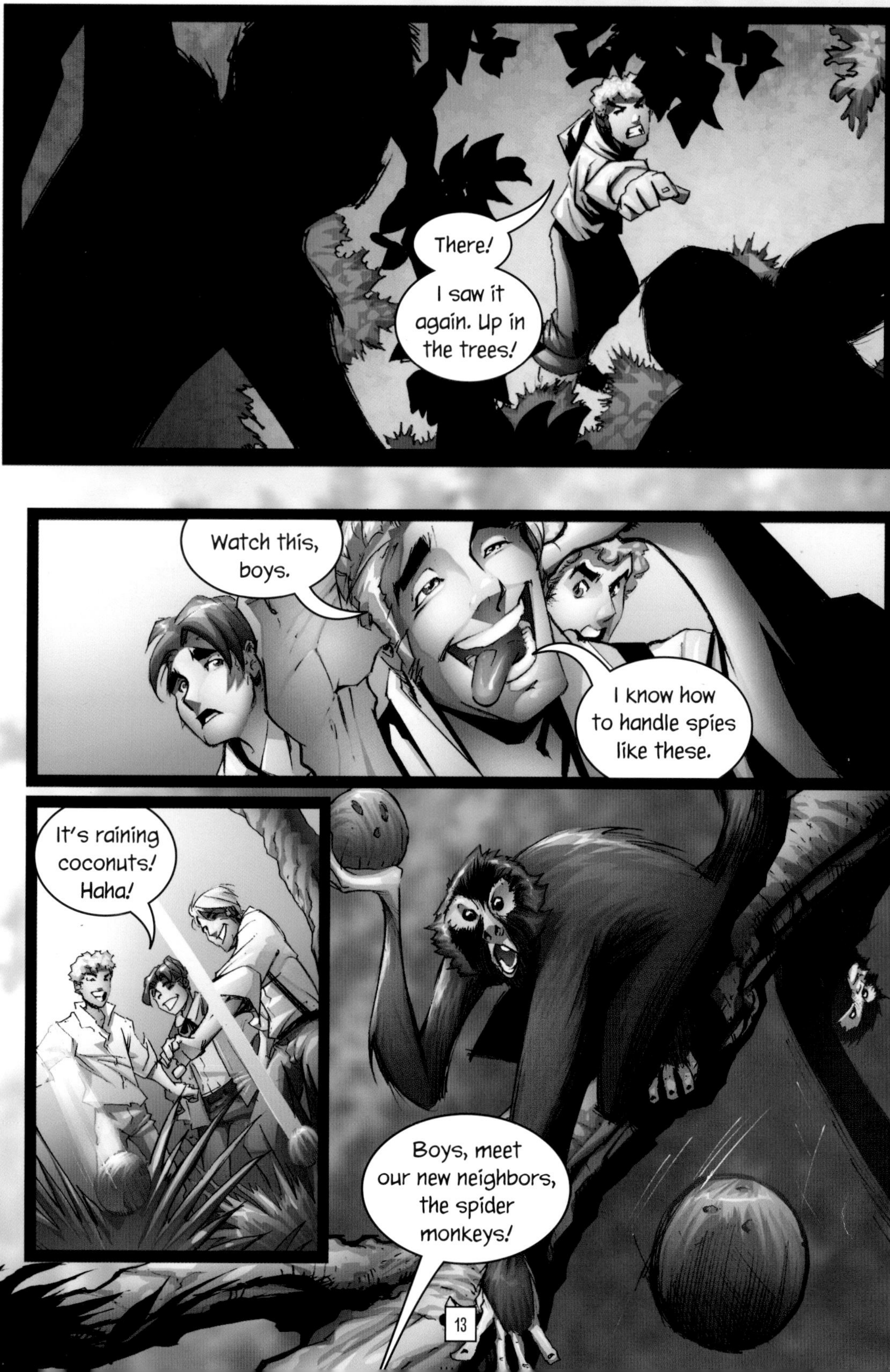
There!
I saw it again. Up in the trees!
Watch this, boys.
I know how to handle spies like these.
It's raining coconuts! Haha!
Boys, meet our new neighbors, the spider monkeys!

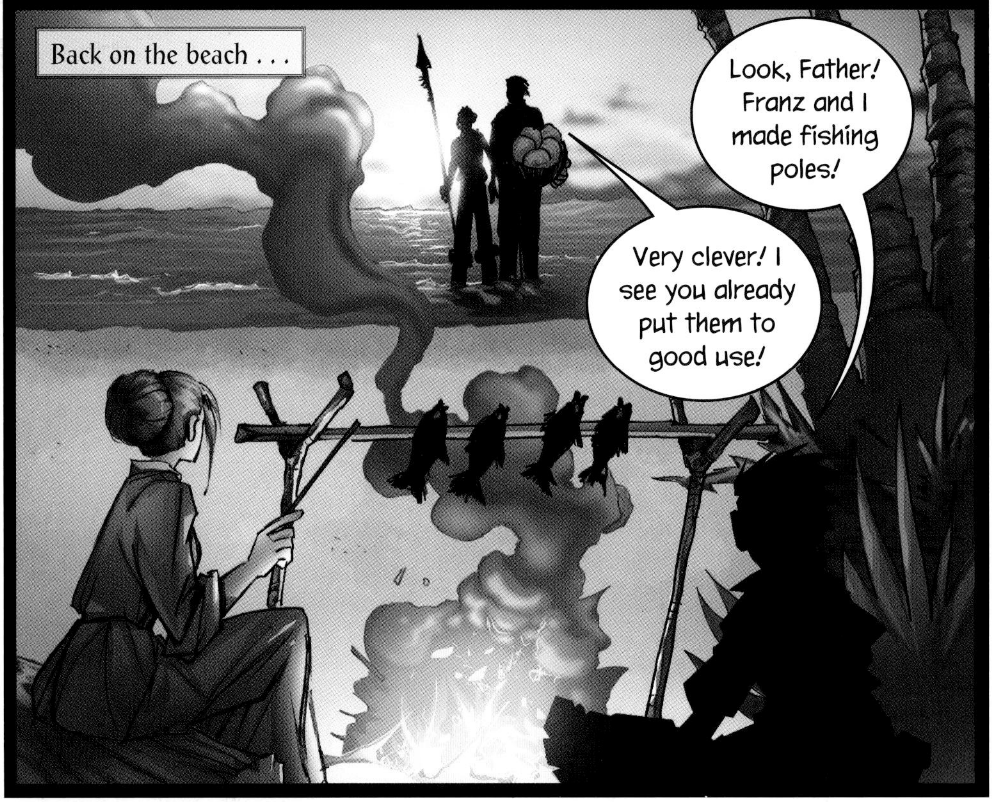
Back on the beach . . .
Look, Father! Franz and I made fishing poles!
Very clever! I see you already put them to good use!

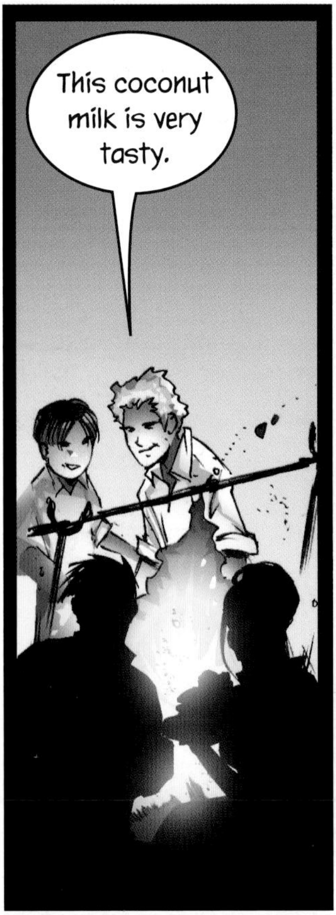
This coconut milk is very tasty.

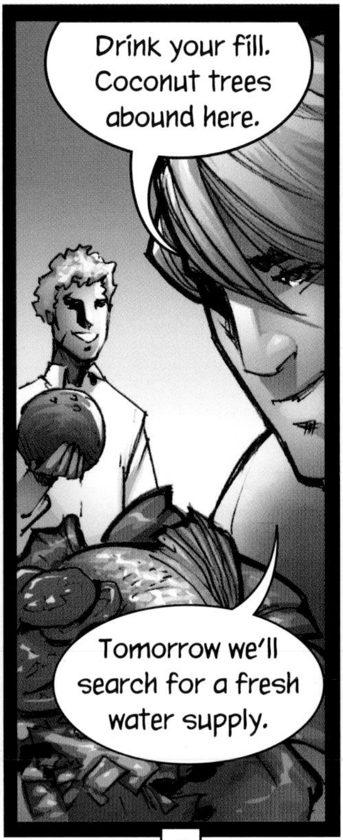
Drink your fill. Coconut trees abound here.
Tomorrow we'll search for a fresh water supply.

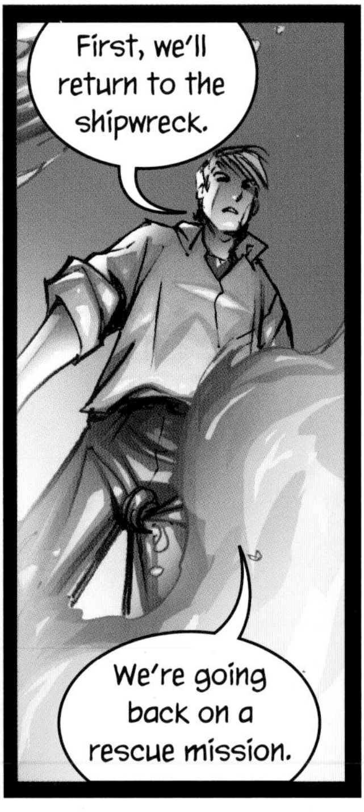
First, we'll return to the shipwreck.
We're going back on a rescue mission.

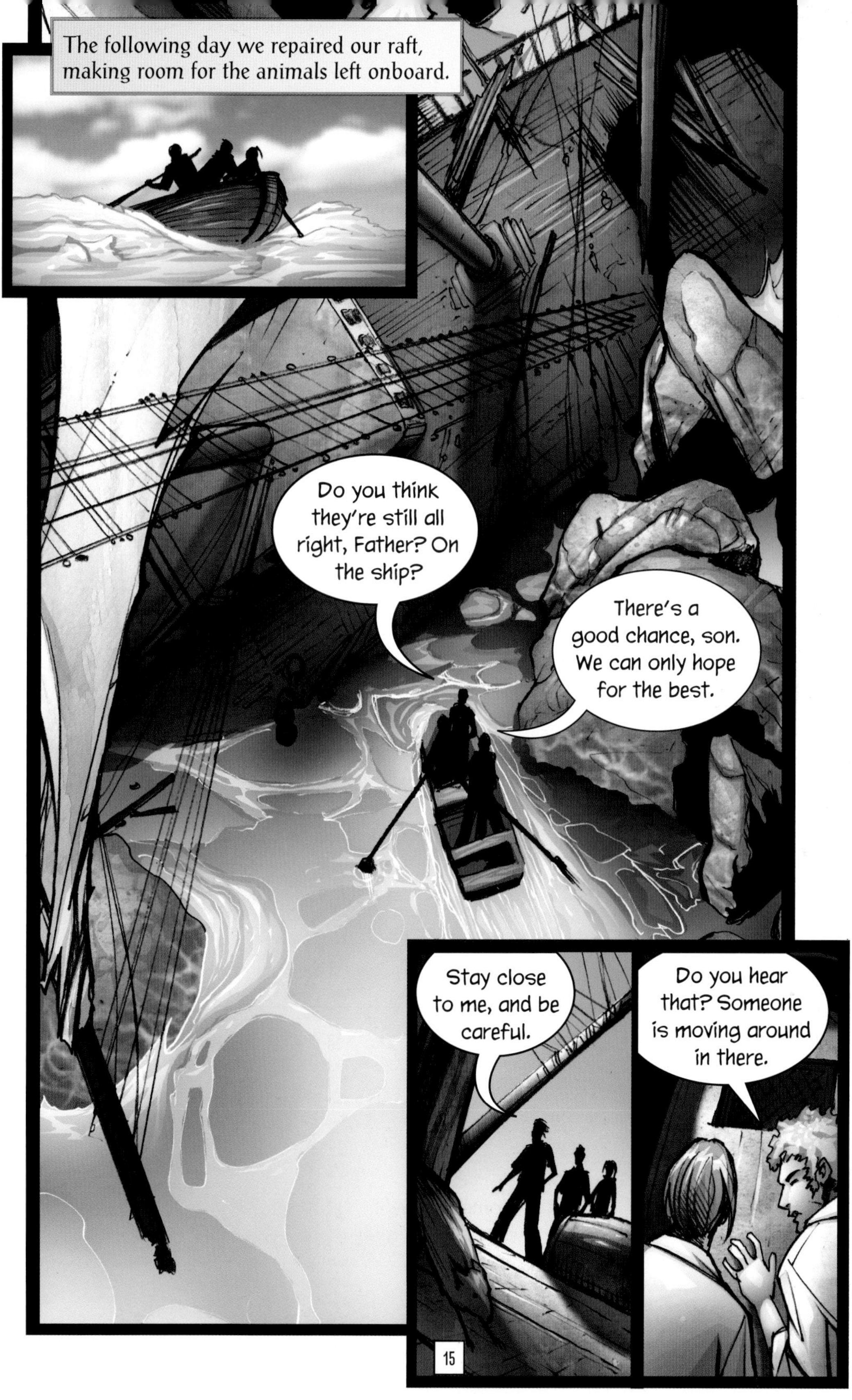
The following day we repaired our raft, making room for the animals left onboard.
Do you think they're still all right, Father? On the ship?
There's a good chance, son. We can only hope for the best.
Stay close to me, and be careful.
Do you hear that? Someone is moving around in there.

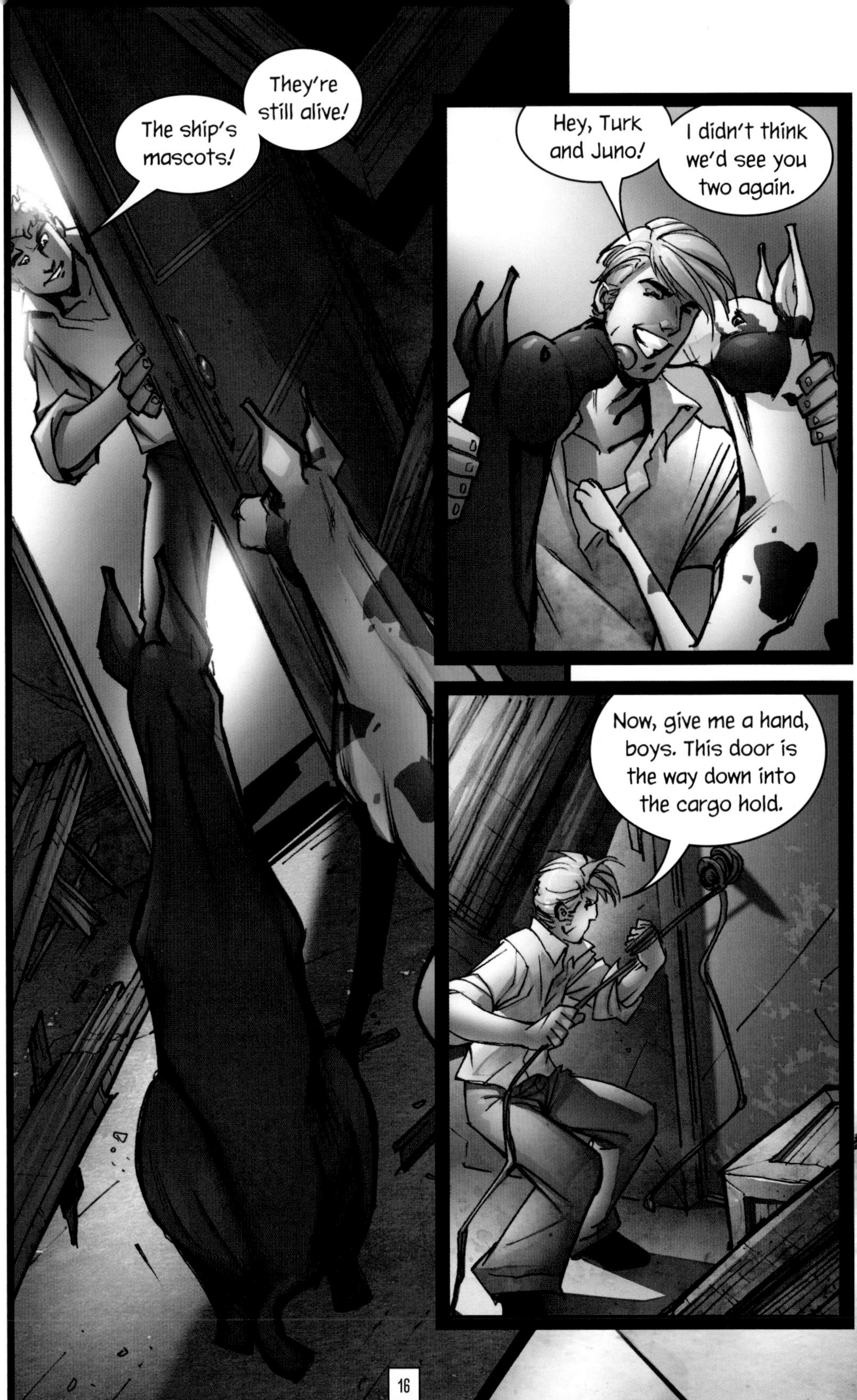
The ship's mascots!
They're still alive!
Hey, Turk and Juno!
I didn't think we'd see you two again.
Now, give me a hand, boys. This door is the way down into the cargo hold.

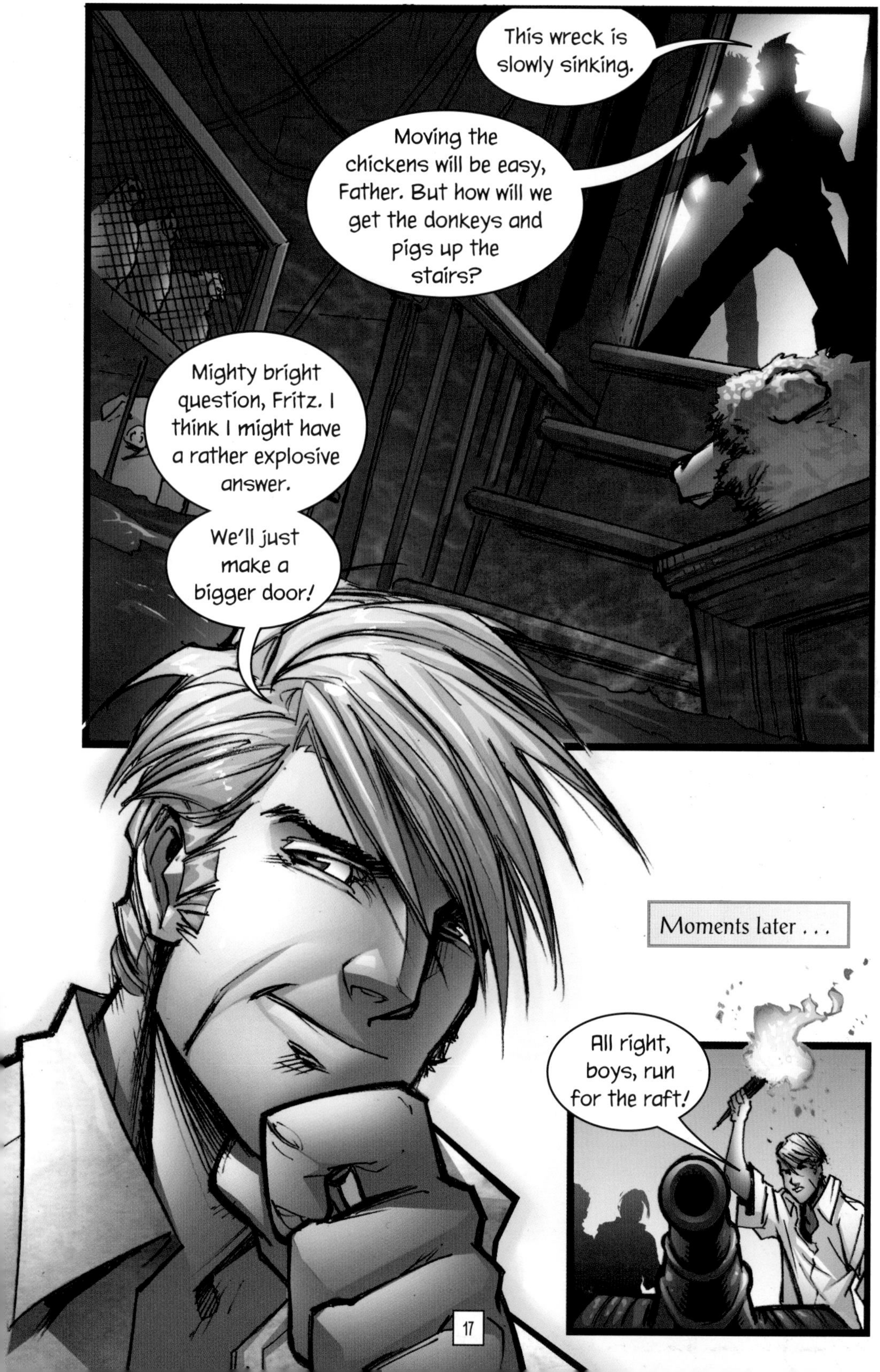
This wreck is slowly sinking.
Moving the chickens will be easy, Father. But how will we get the donkeys and pigs up the stairs?
Mighty bright question, Fritz. I think I might have a rather explosive answer.
We'll just make a bigger door!
Moments later . . .
All right, boys, run for the raft!

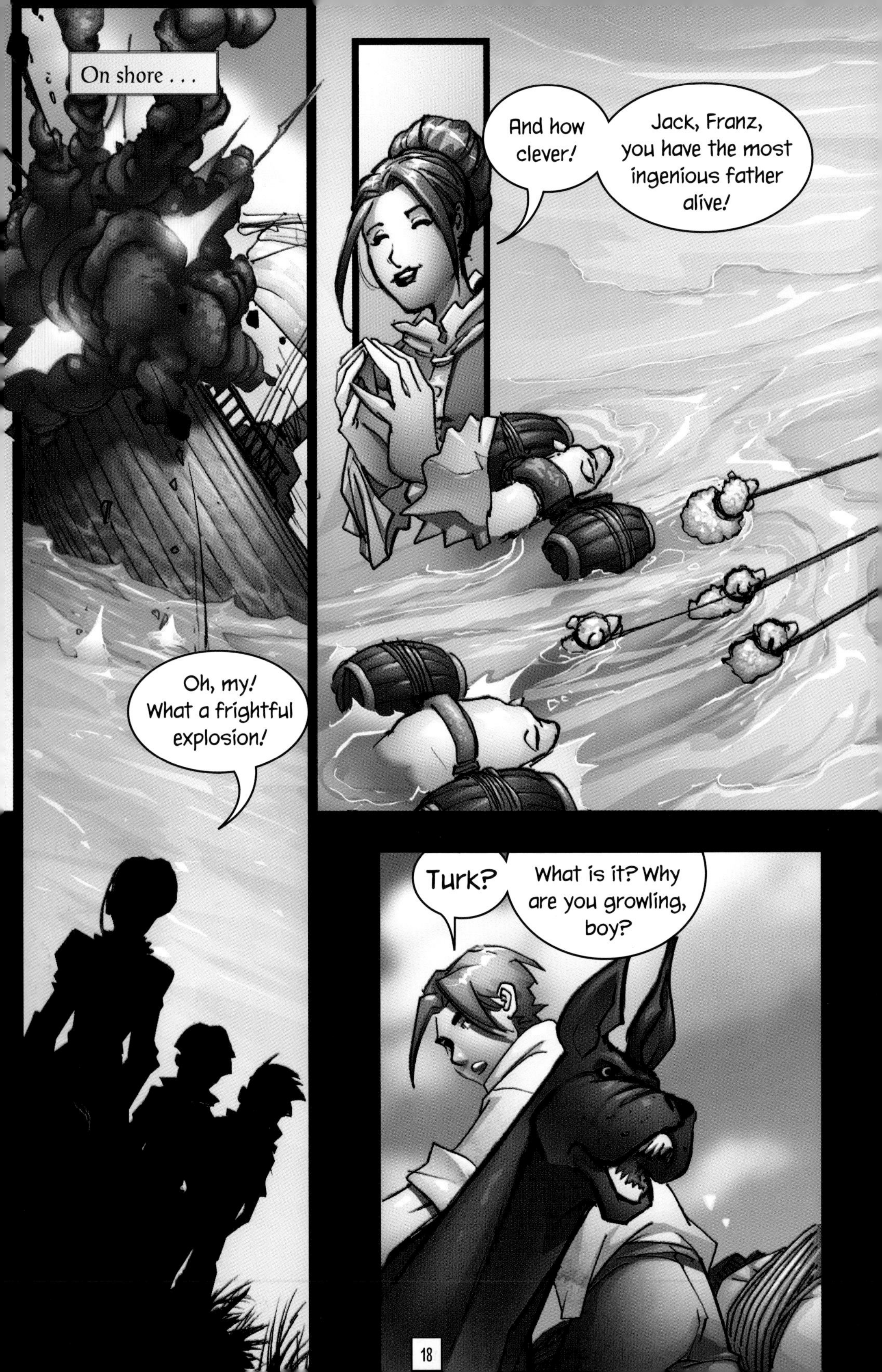
On shore . . .
Oh, my! What a frightful explosion!
And how clever!
Jack, Franz, you have the most ingenious father alive!
Turk?
What is it? Why are you growling, boy?

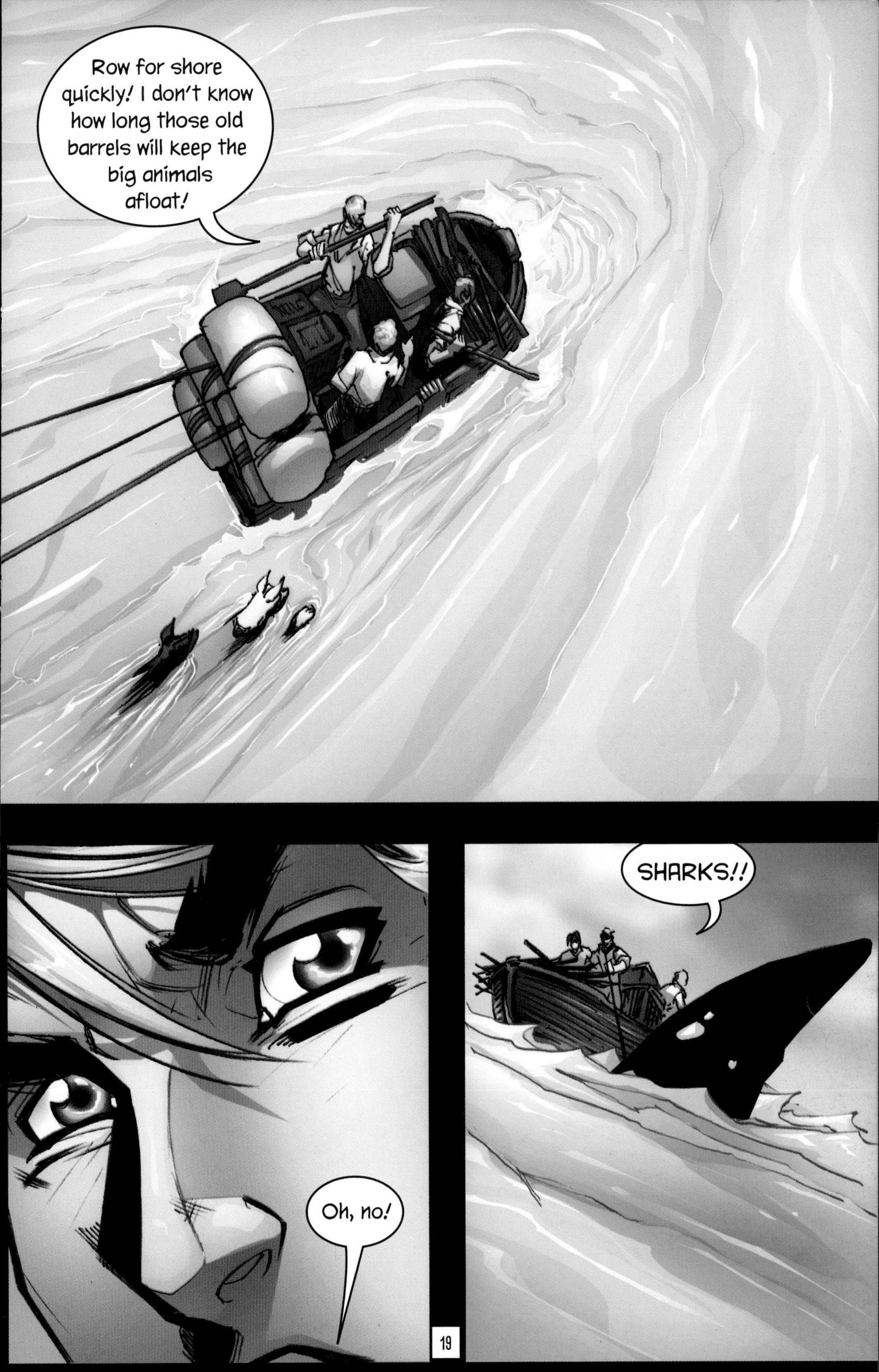
Row for shore quickly! I don't know how long those old barrels will keep the big animals afloat!
Oh, no!
SHARKS!!

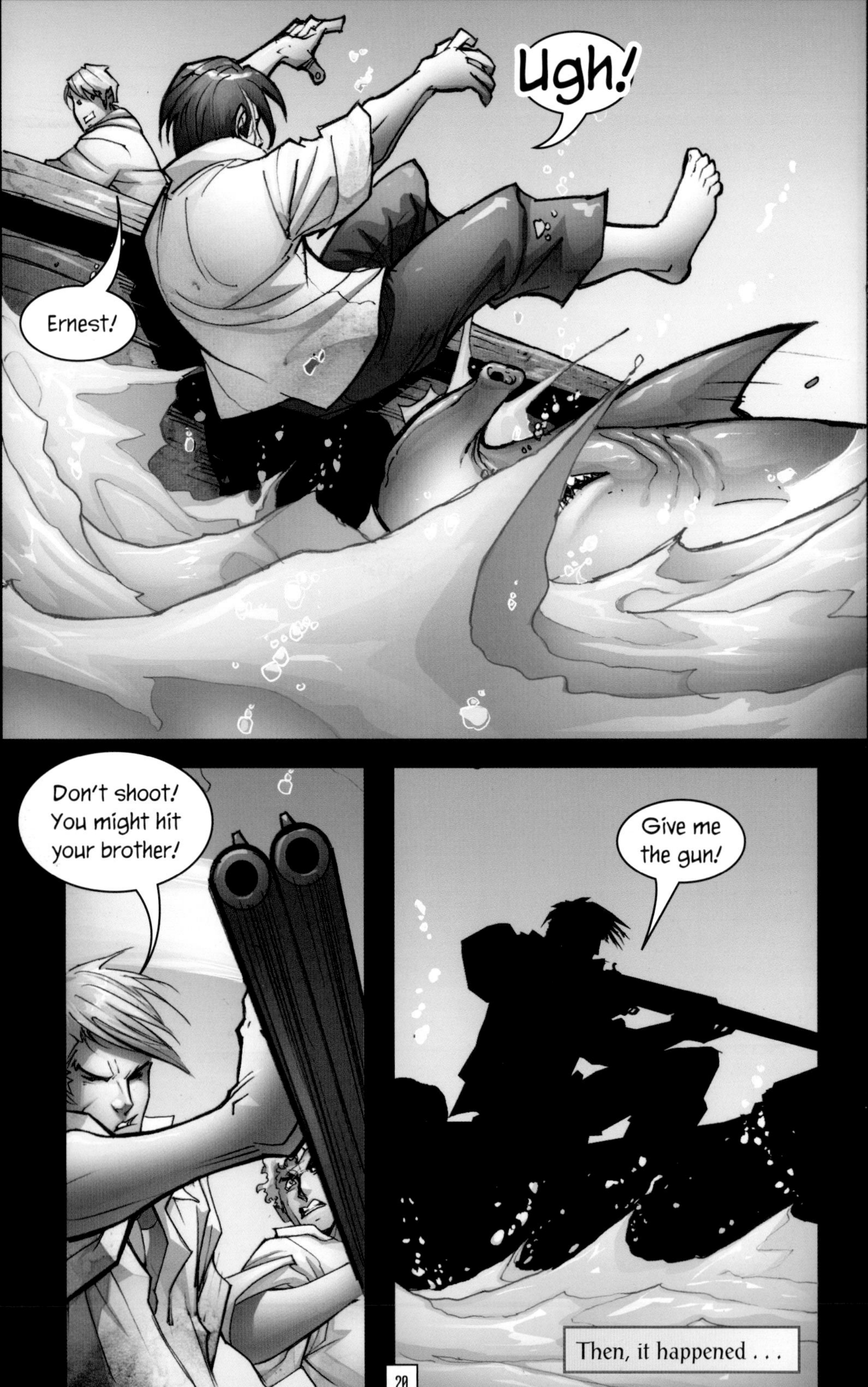
Ugh!
Ernest!
Don't shoot! You might hit your brother!
Give me the gun!
Then, it happened . . .

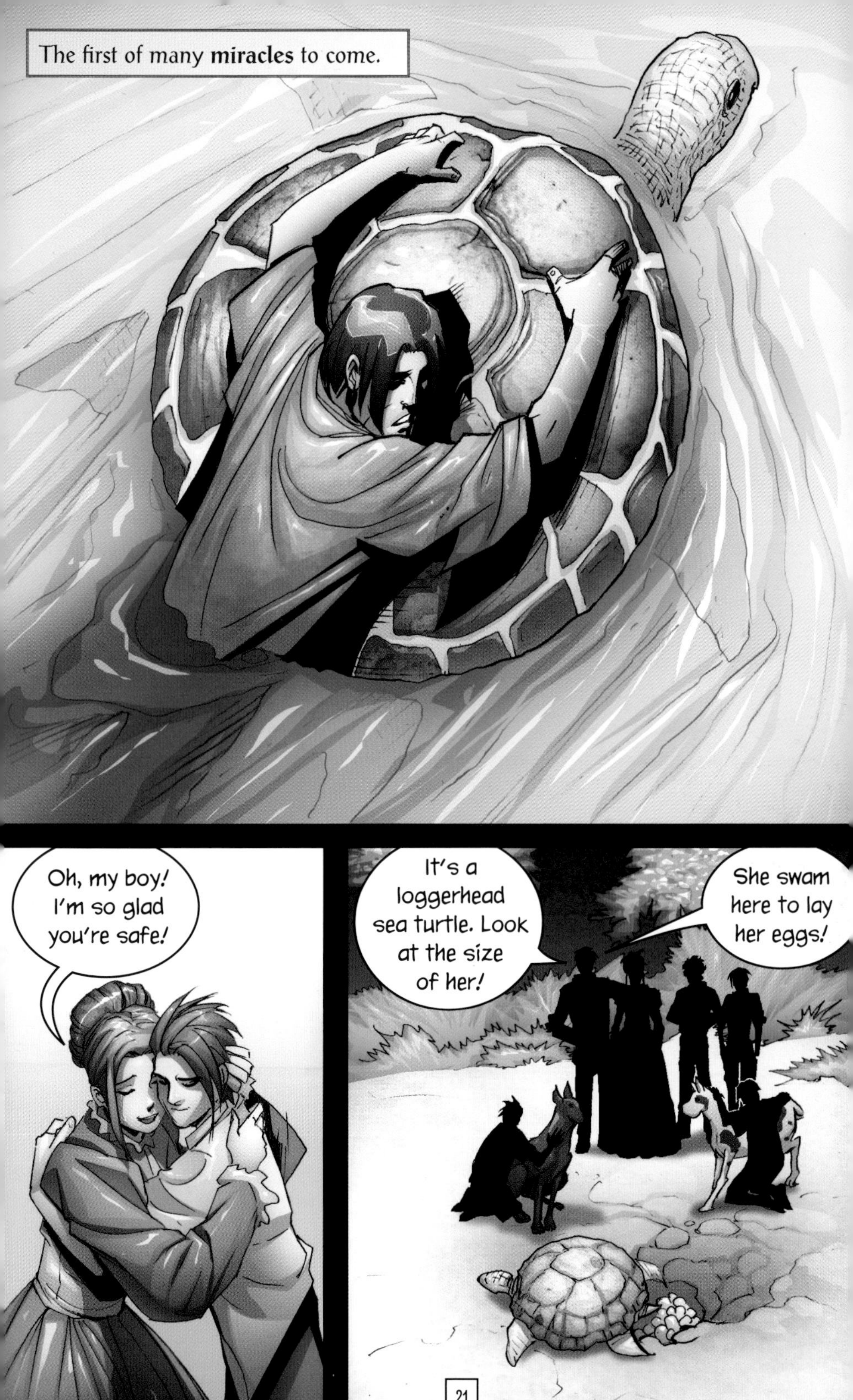
The first of many **miracles** to come.
Oh, my boy! I'm so glad you're safe!
It's a loggerhead sea turtle. Look at the size of her!
She swam here to lay her eggs!

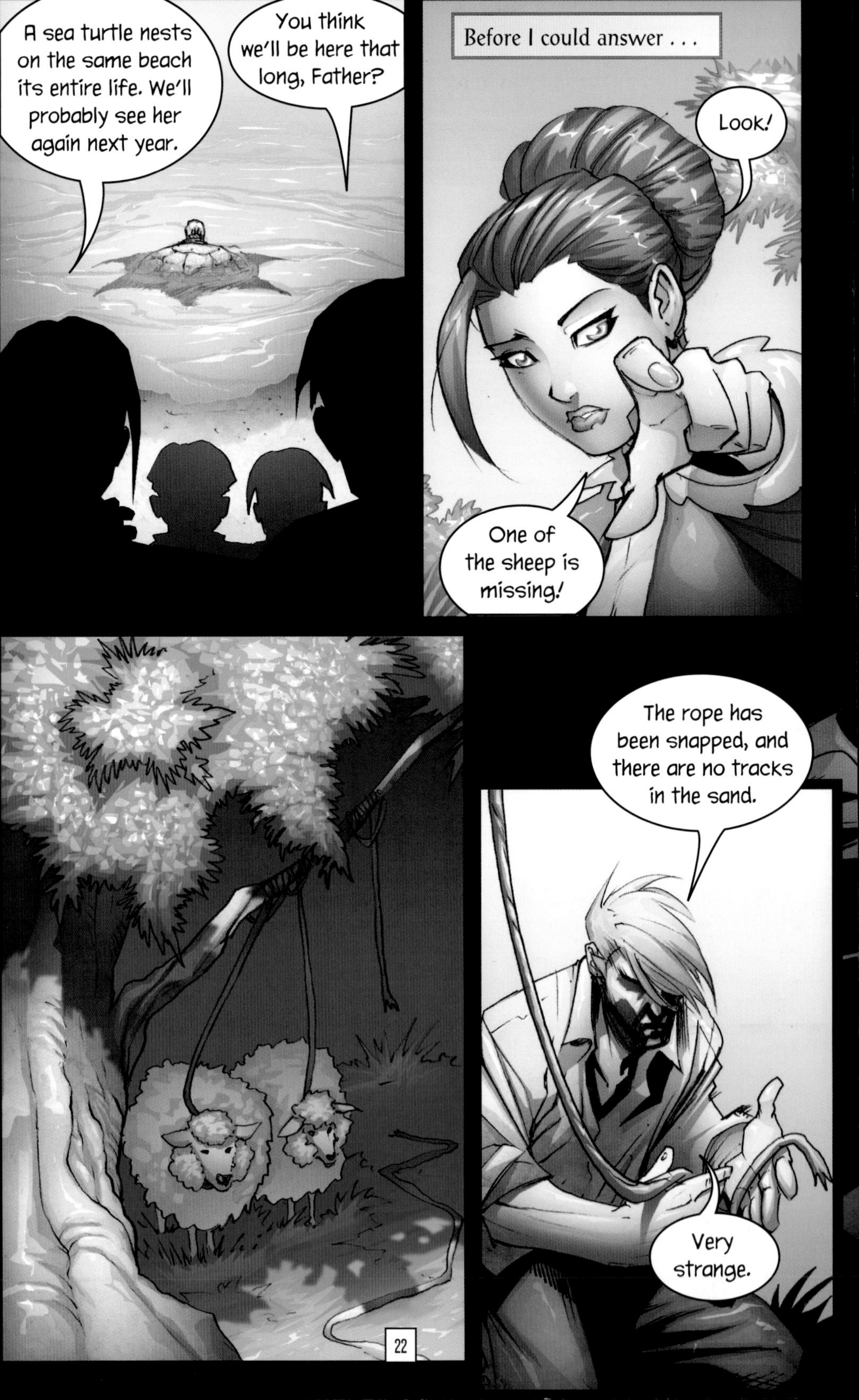
A sea turtle nests on the same beach its entire life. We'll probably see her again next year.
You think we'll be here that long, Father?
Before I could answer . . .
Look!
One of the sheep is missing!
The rope has been snapped, and there are no tracks in the sand.
Very strange.

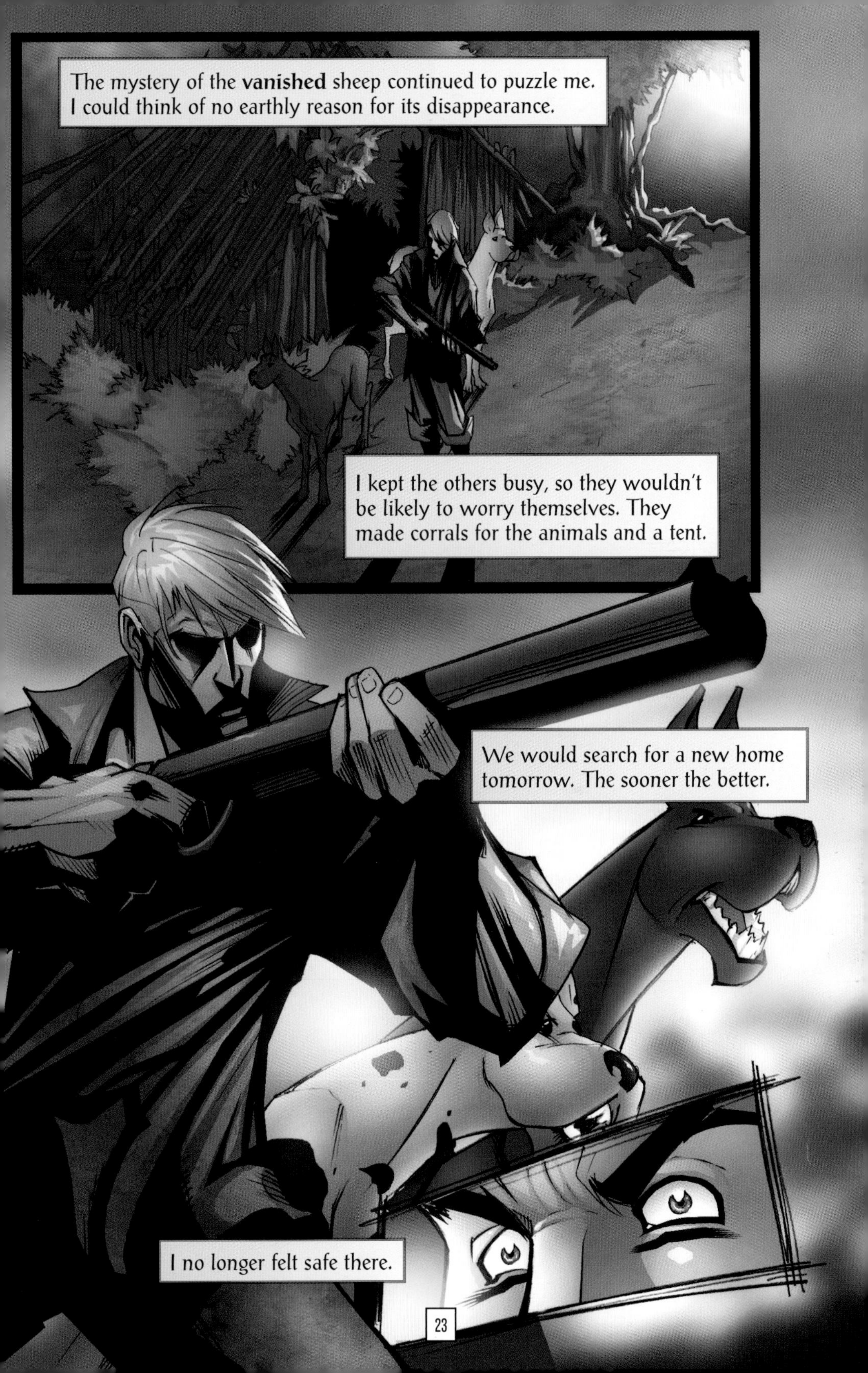
The mystery of the **vanished** sheep continued to puzzle me. I could think of no earthly reason for its disappearance.
I kept the others busy, so they wouldn't be likely to worry themselves. They made corrals for the animals and a tent.
We would search for a new home tomorrow. The sooner the better.
I no longer felt safe there.

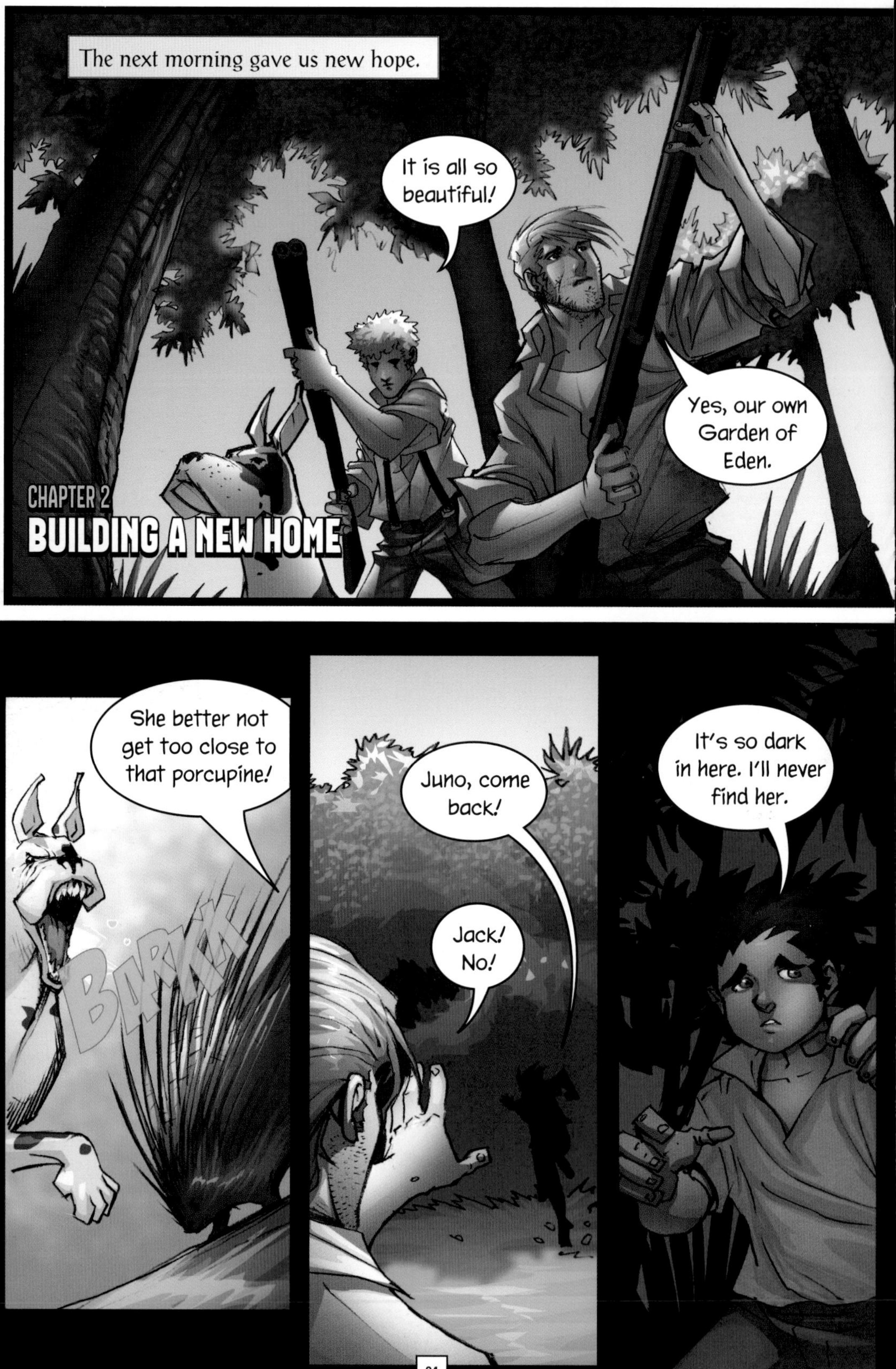
The next morning gave us new hope.
It is all so beautiful!
Yes, our own Garden of Eden.
CHAPTER 2
BUILDING A NEW HOME
She better not get too close to that porcupine!
BARK
Juno, come back!
Jack! No!
It's so dark in here. I'll never find her.

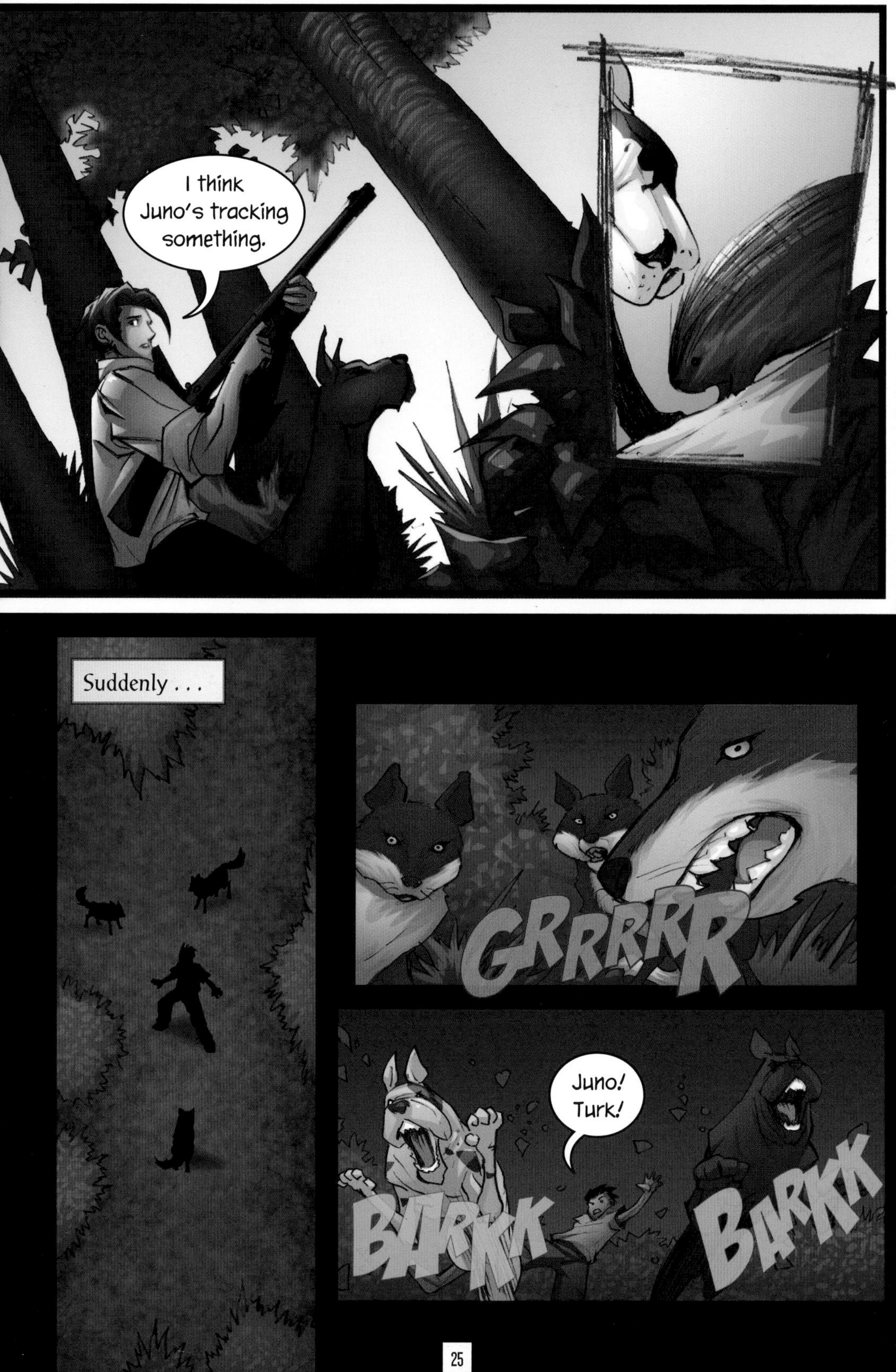
I think Juno's tracking something.
Suddenly . . .
GRRRRR
Juno! Turk!
BARKK
BARKK

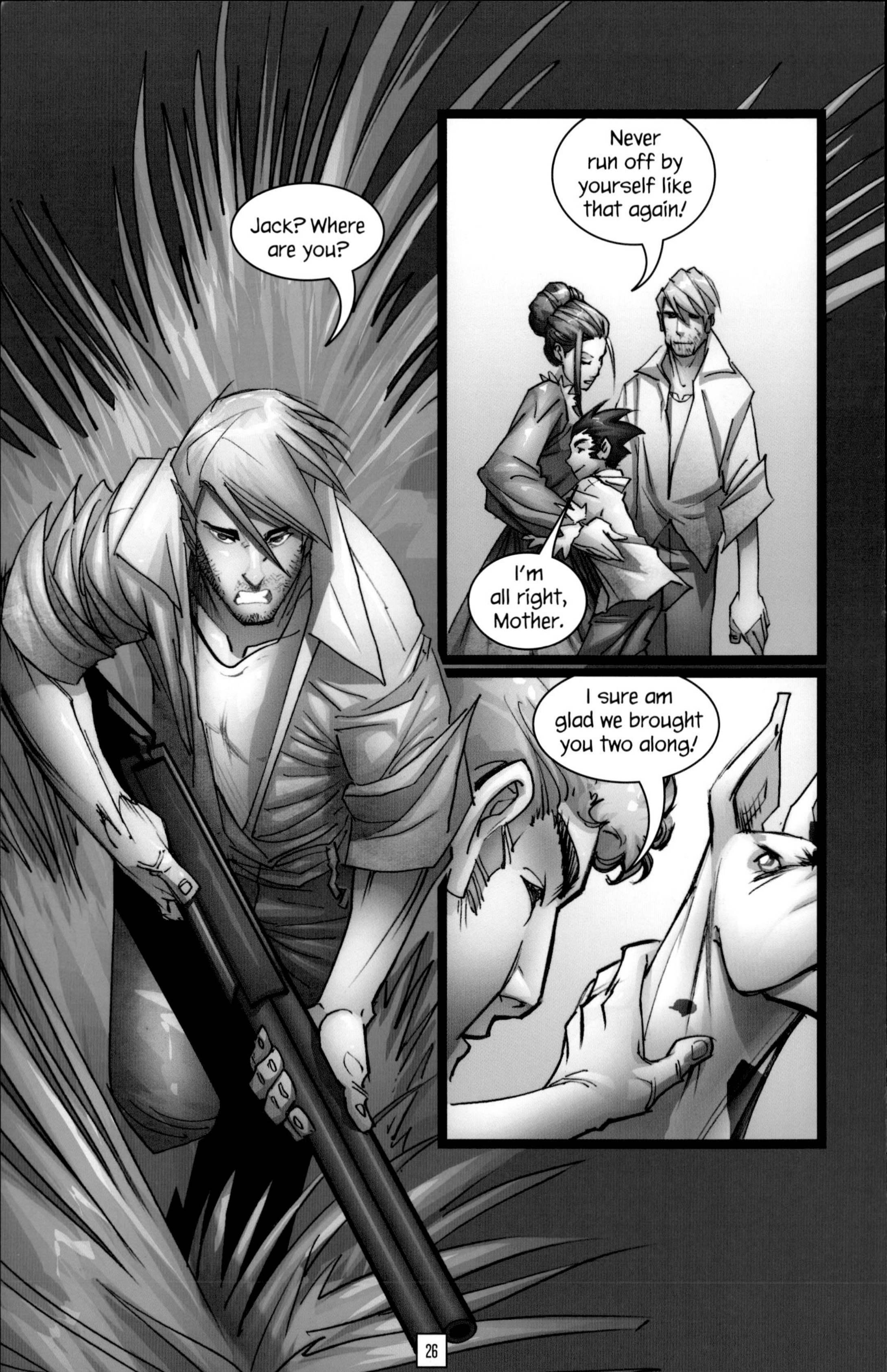
Jack? Where are you?
Never run off by yourself like that again!
I'm all right, Mother.
I sure am glad we brought you two along!

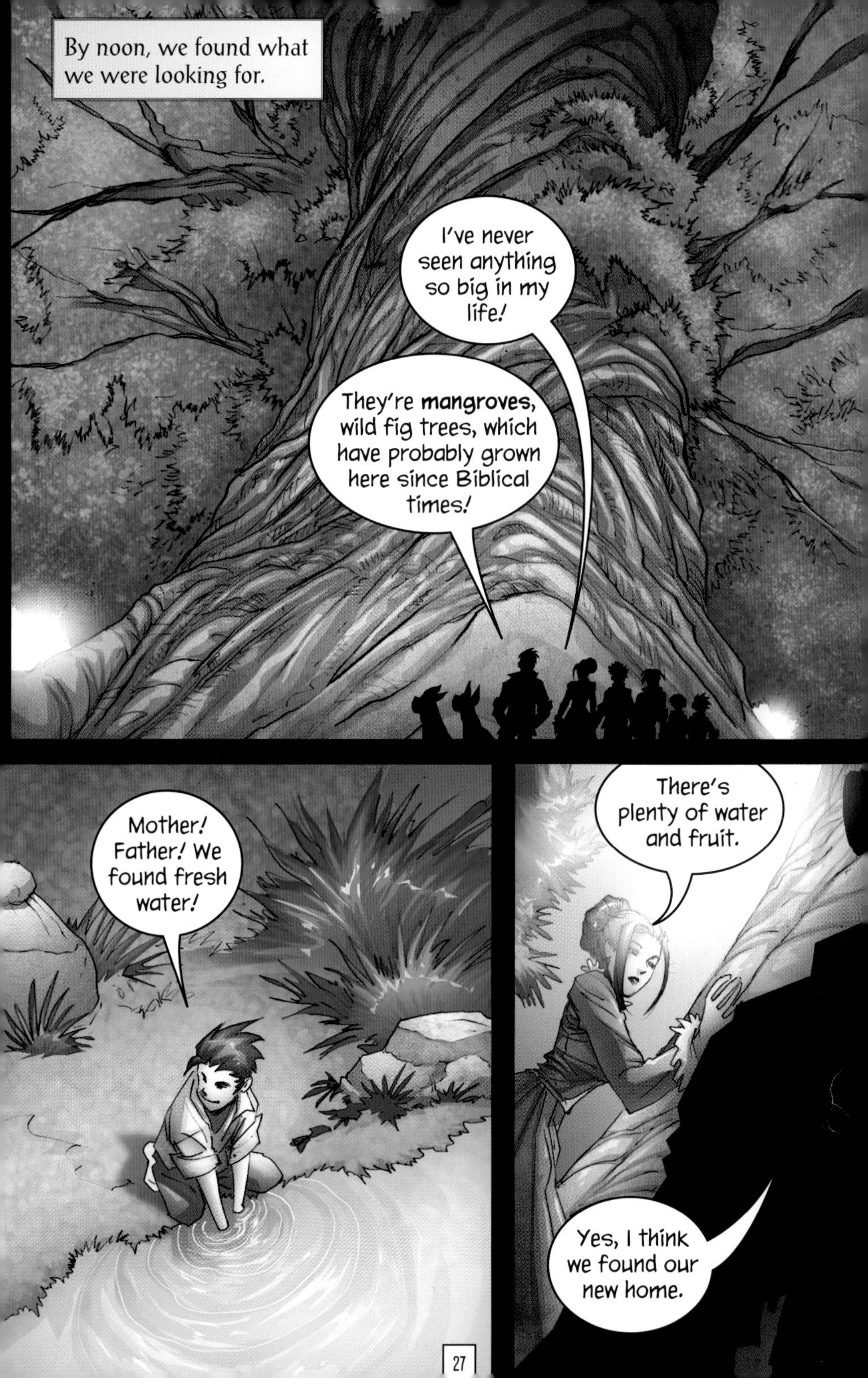
By noon, we found what we were looking for.
I've never seen anything so big in my life!
They're **mangroves**, wild fig trees, which have probably grown here since Biblical times!
Mother! Father! We found fresh water!
There's plenty of water and fruit.
Yes, I think we found our new home.

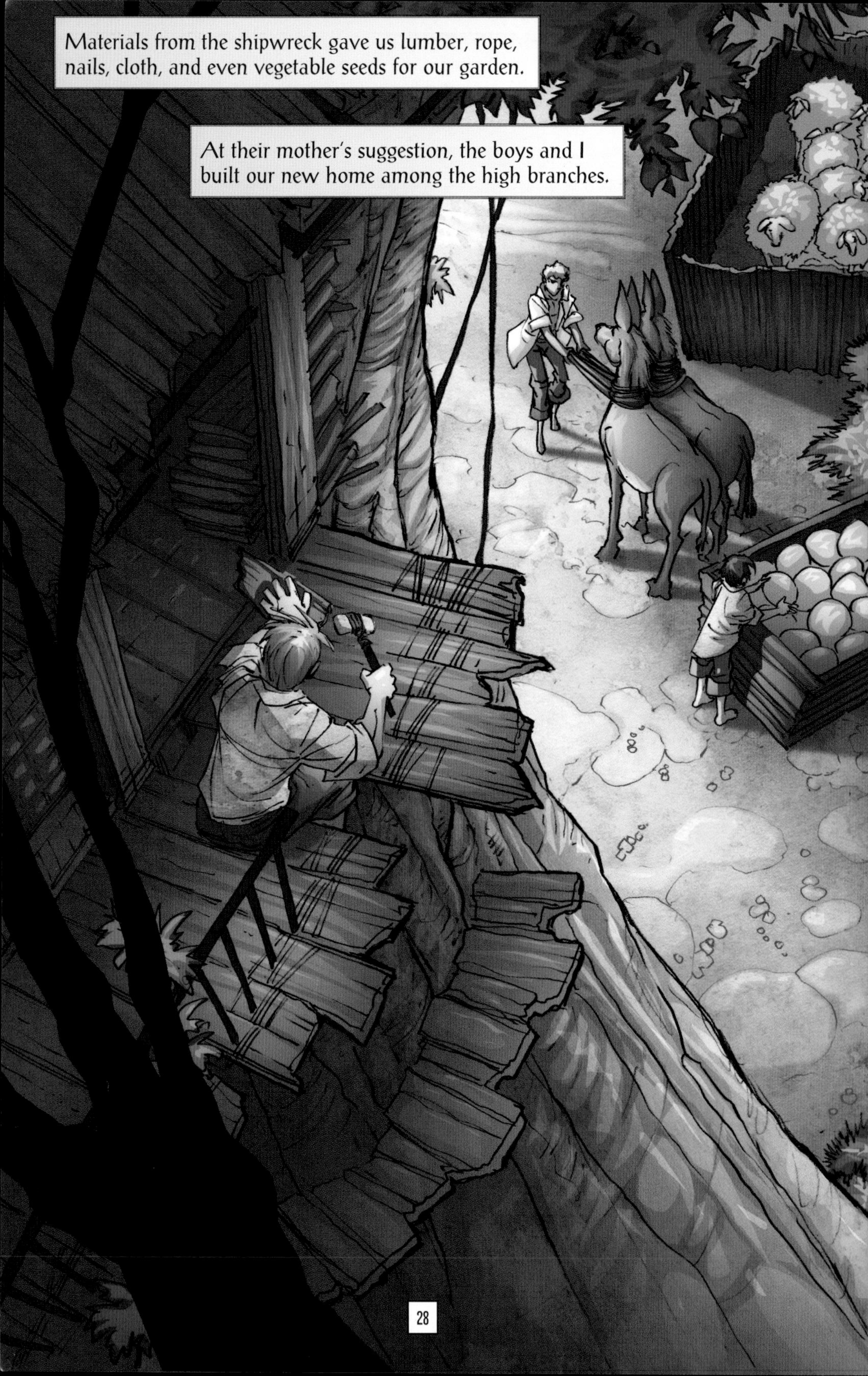
Materials from the shipwreck gave us lumber, rope, nails, cloth, and even vegetable seeds for our garden.
At their mother's suggestion, the boys and I built our new home among the high branches.

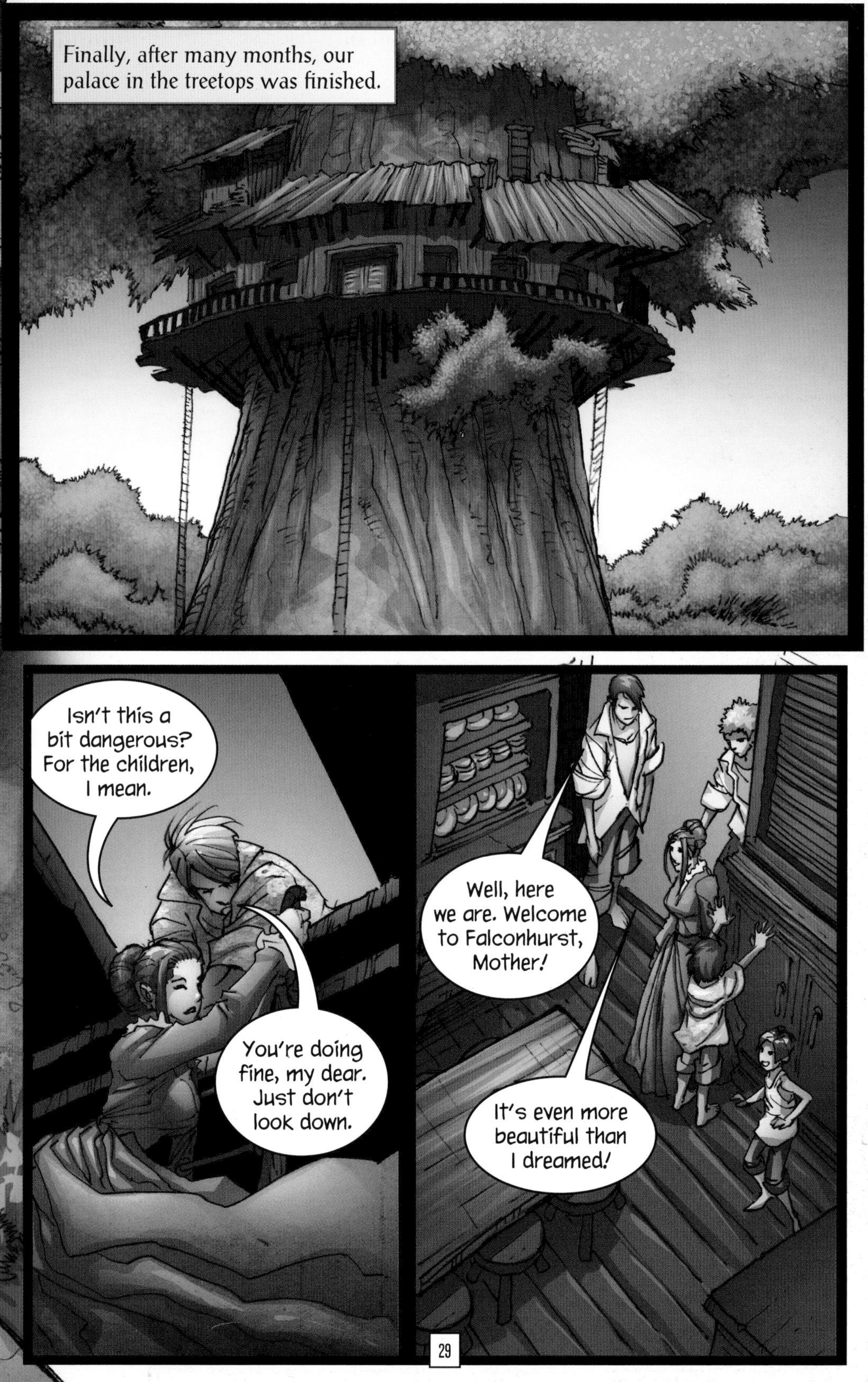

Finally, after many months, our palace in the treetops was finished.
Isn't this a bit dangerous? For the children, I mean.
You're doing fine, my dear. Just don't look down.
Well, here we are. Welcome to Falconhurst, Mother!
It's even more beautiful than I dreamed!

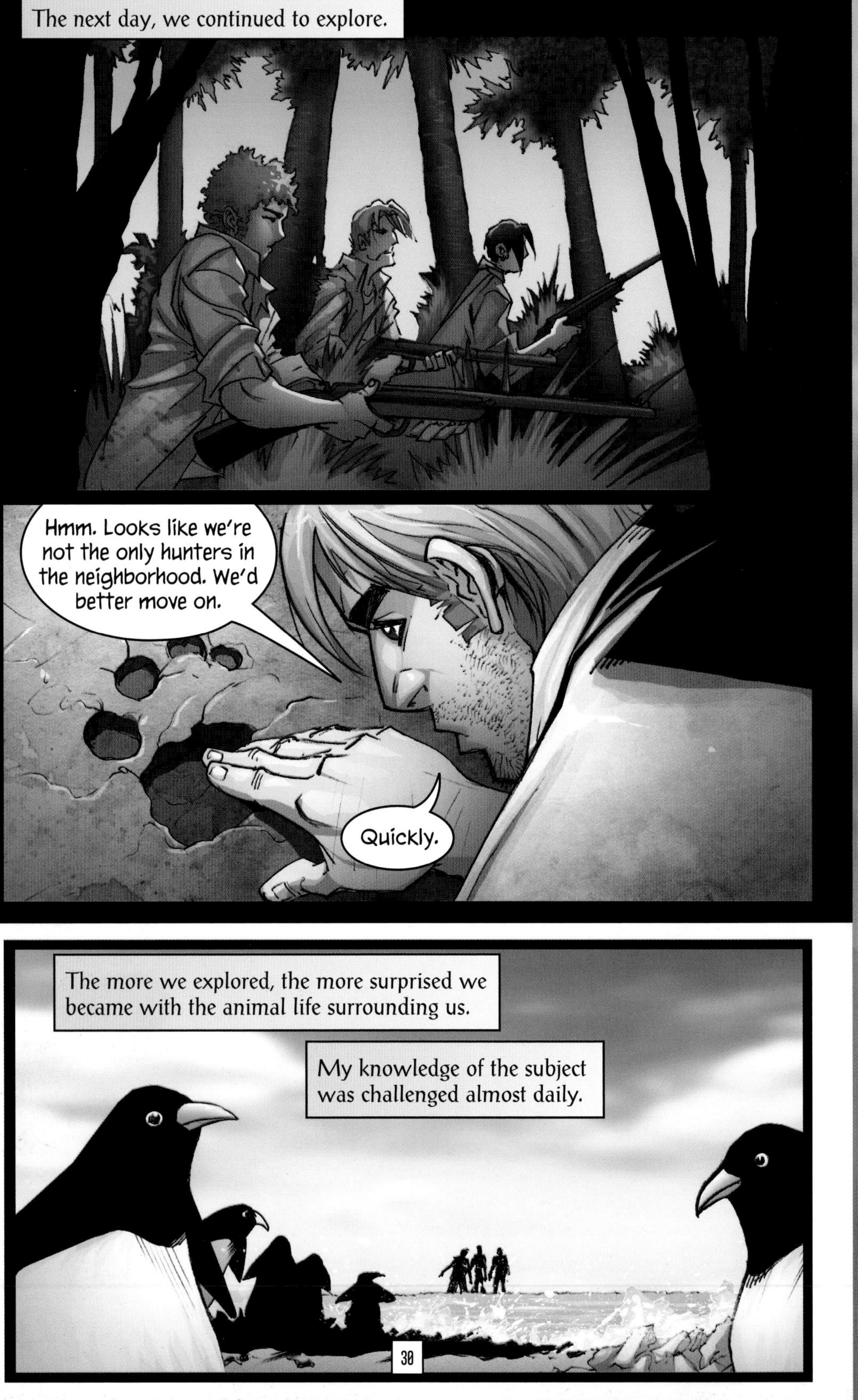
The next day, we continued to explore.
Hmm. Looks like we're not the only hunters in the neighborhood. We'd better move on.
Quickly.
The more we explored, the more surprised we became with the animal life surrounding us.
My knowledge of the subject was challenged almost daily.

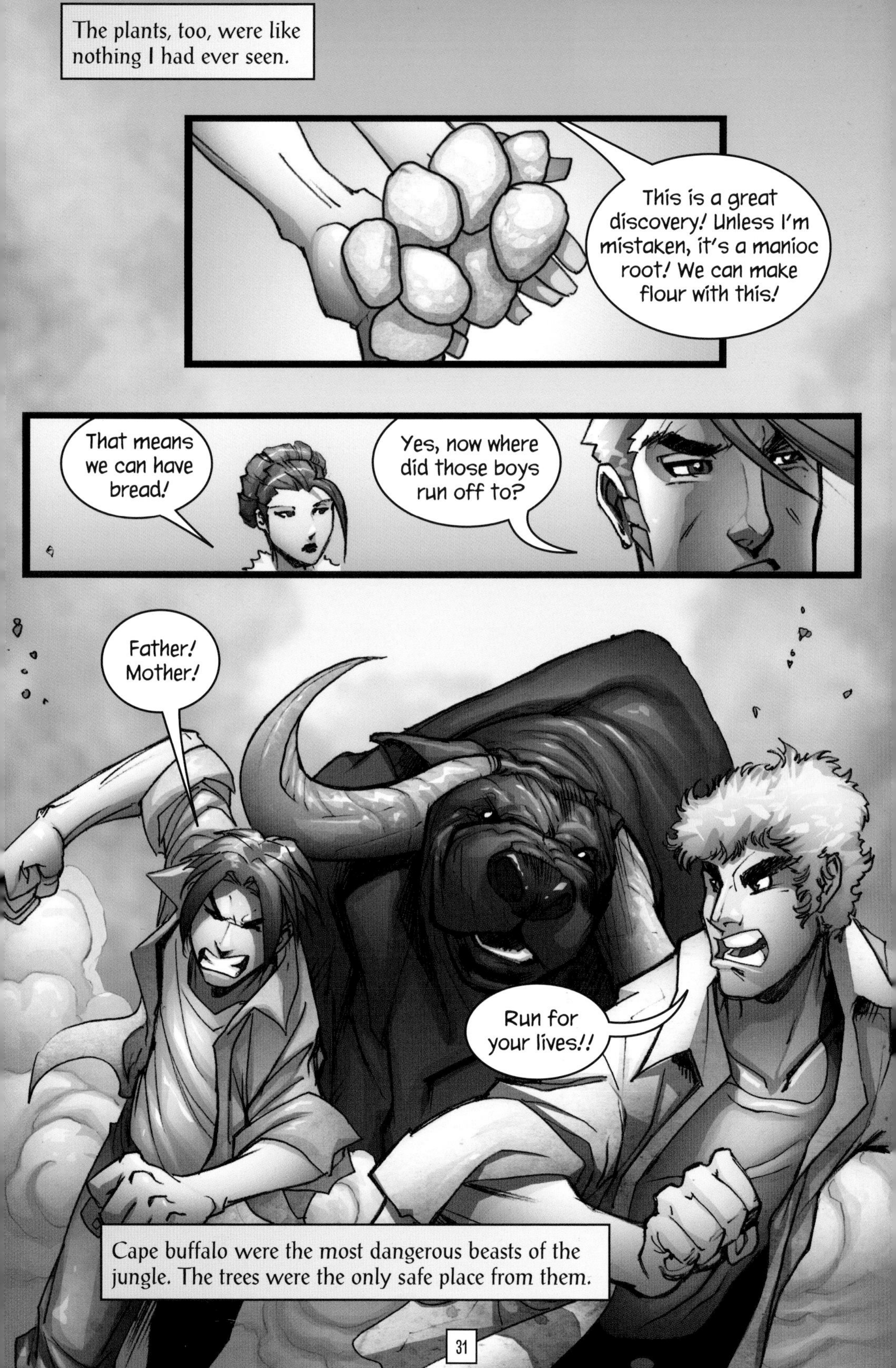
The plants, too, were like nothing I had ever seen.
This is a great discovery! Unless I'm mistaken, it's a manioc root! We can make flour with this!
That means we can have bread!
Yes, now where did those boys run off to?
Father! Mother!
Run for your lives!!
Cape buffalo were the most dangerous beasts of the jungle. The trees were the only safe place from them.

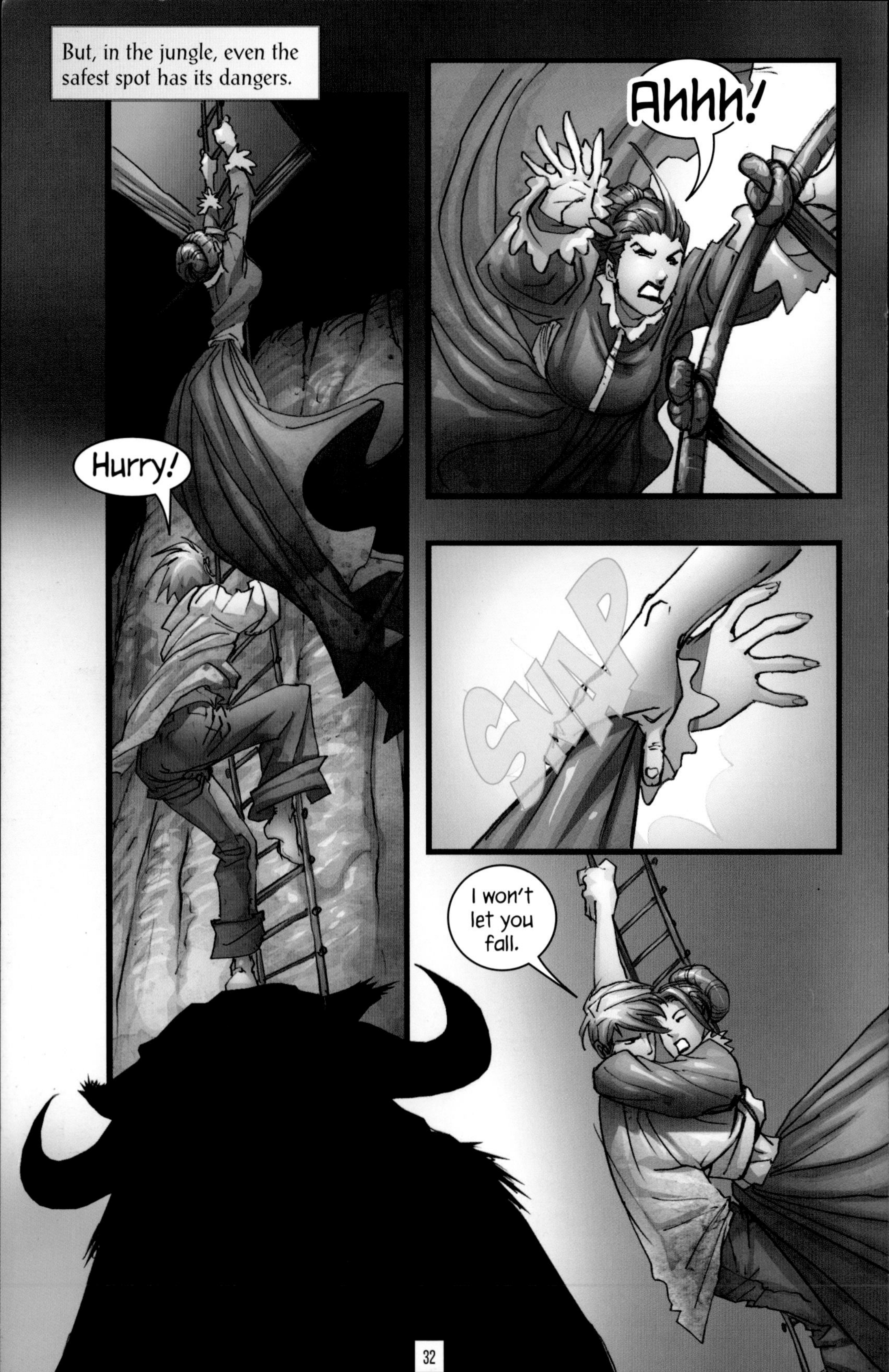
But, in the jungle, even the safest spot has its dangers.
Ahhh!
Hurry!
SNAP
I won't let you fall.

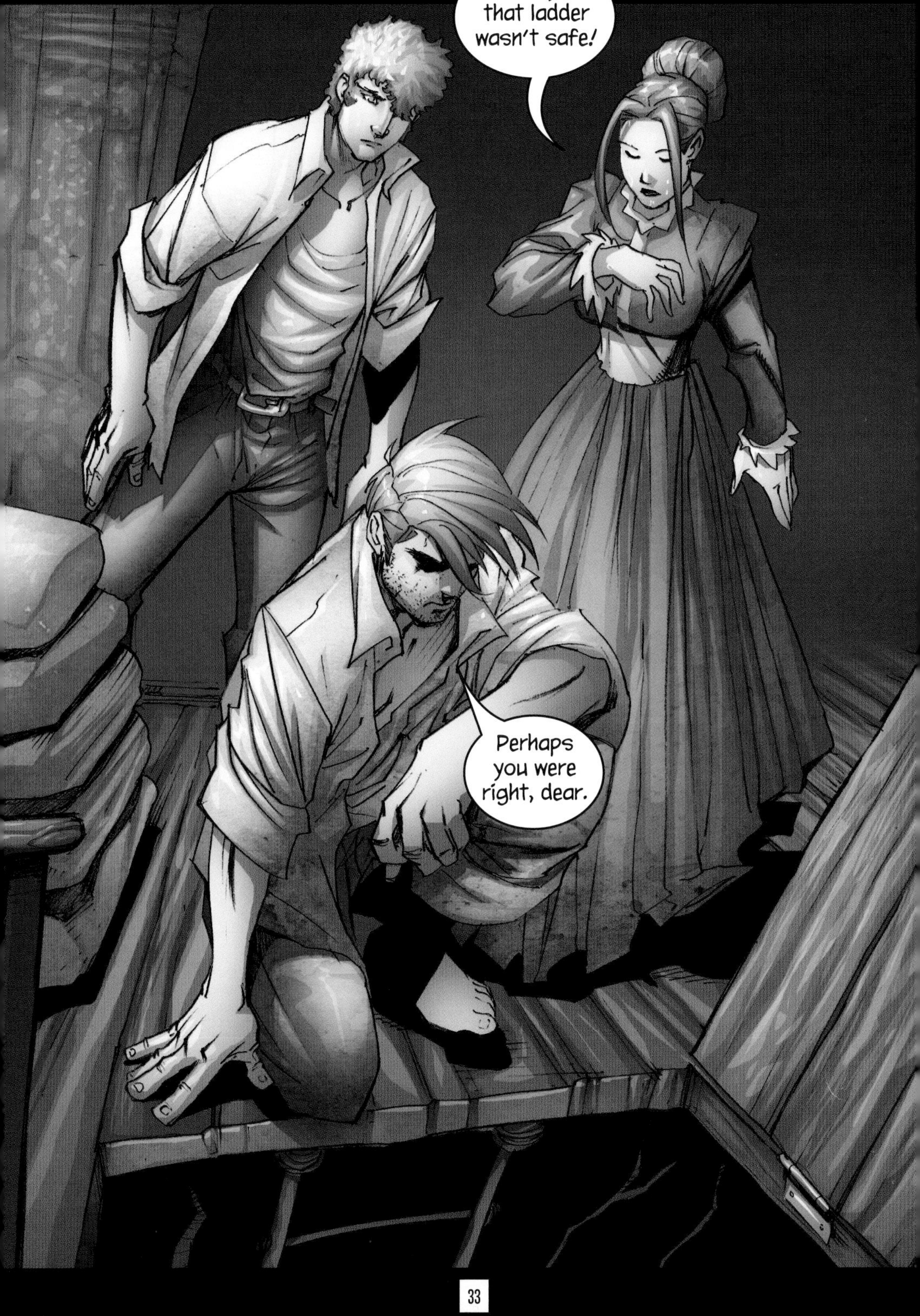
I told you that ladder wasn't safe!
Perhaps you were right, dear.

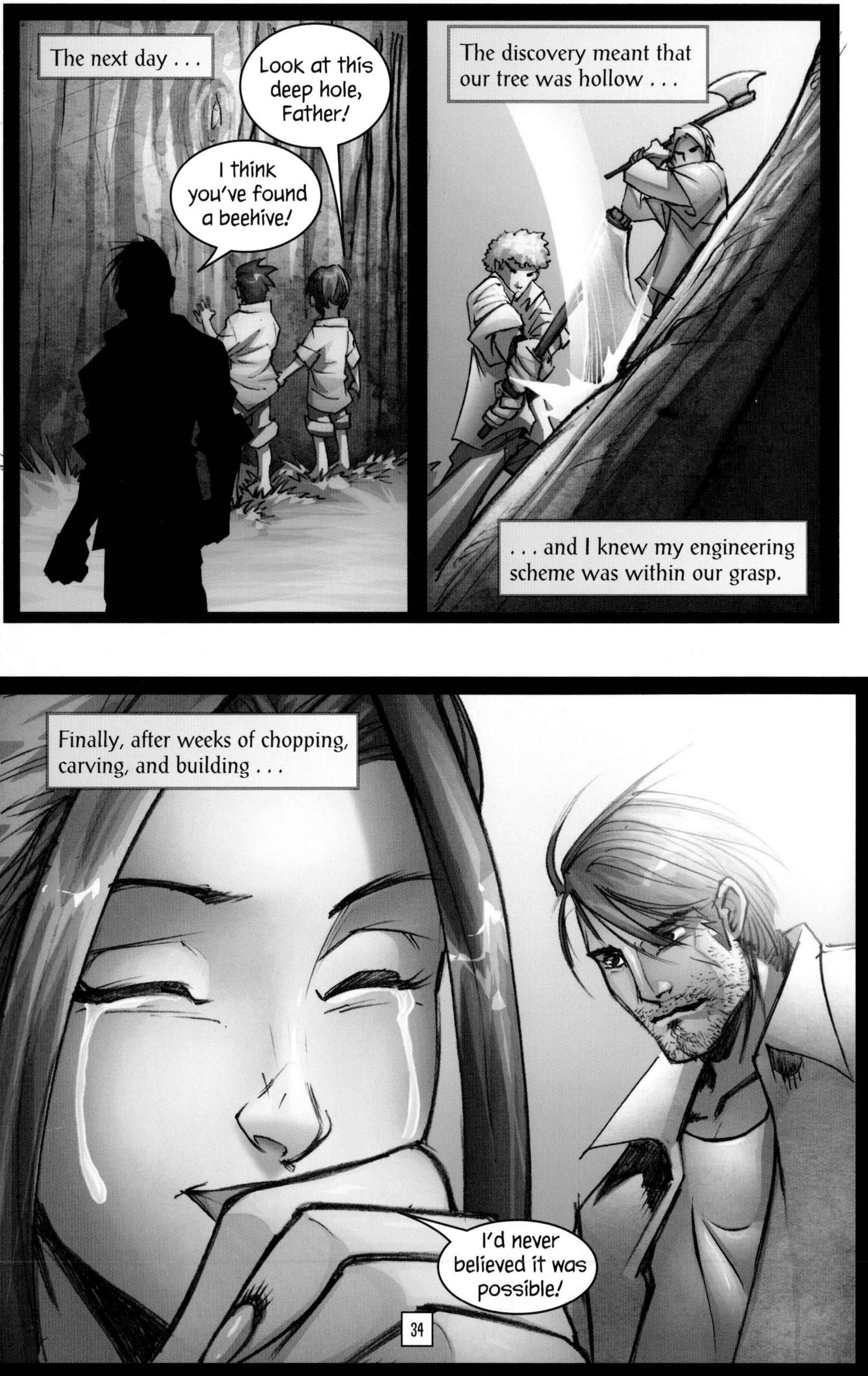
The next day . . .
Look at this deep hole, Father!
I think you've found a beehive!
The discovery meant that our tree was hollow . . .
. . . and I knew my engineering scheme was within our grasp.
Finally, after weeks of chopping, carving, and building . . .
I'd never believed it was possible!

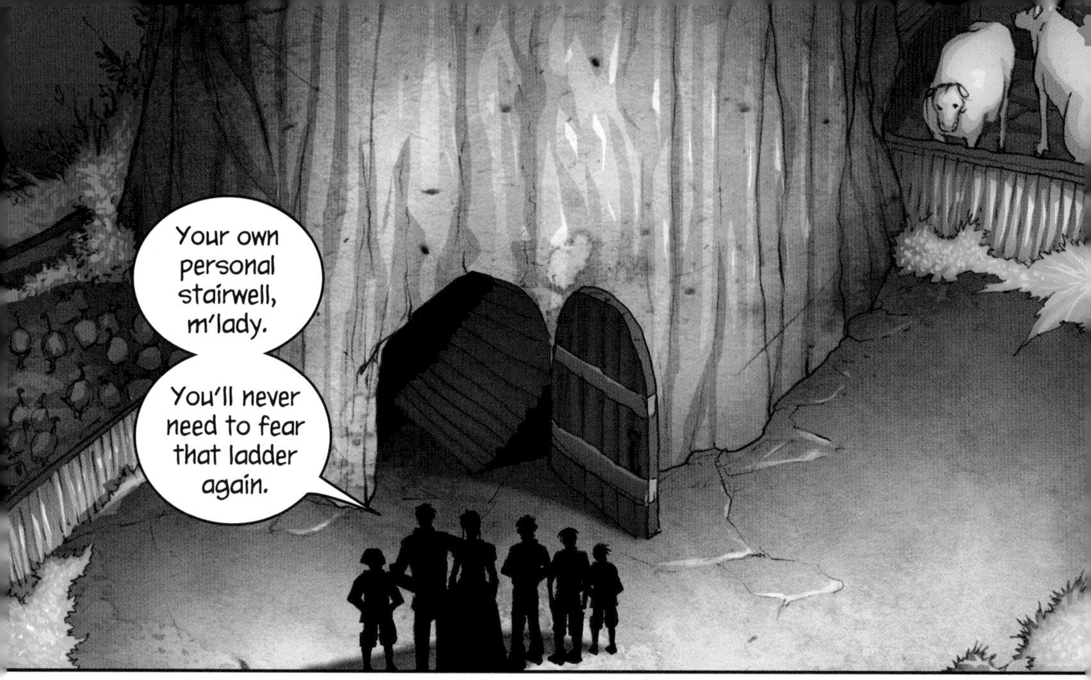
Your own personal stairwell, m'lady.
You'll never need to fear that ladder again.

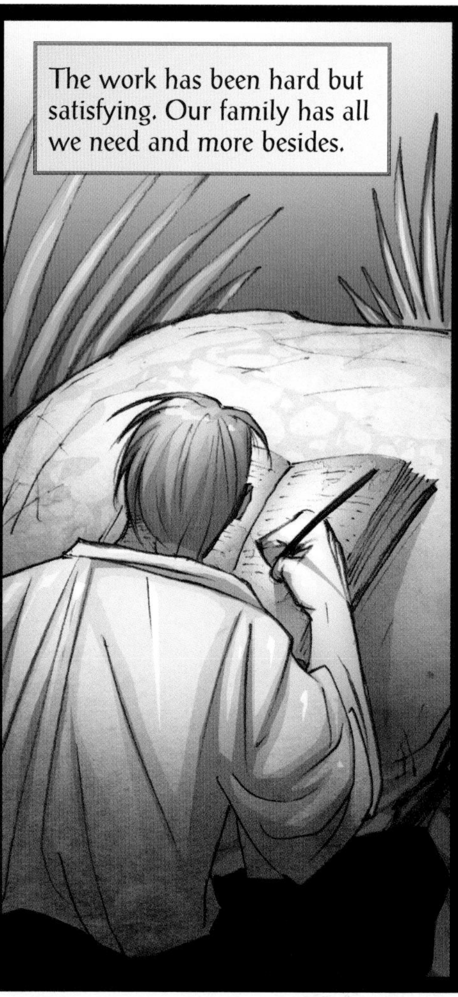
The work has been hard but satisfying. Our family has all we need and more besides.

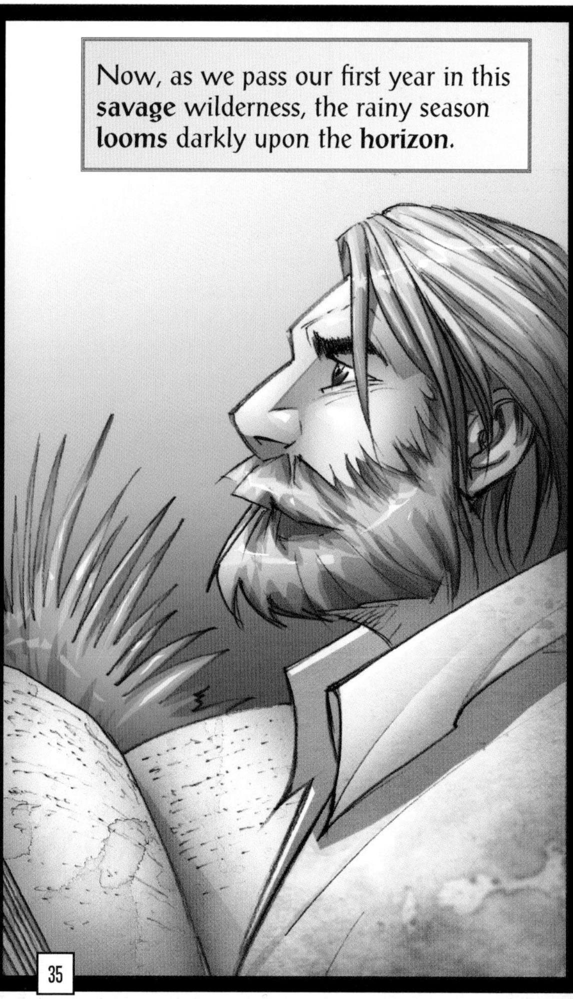
Now, as we pass our first year in this **savage** wilderness, the rainy season **looms** darkly upon the **horizon**.

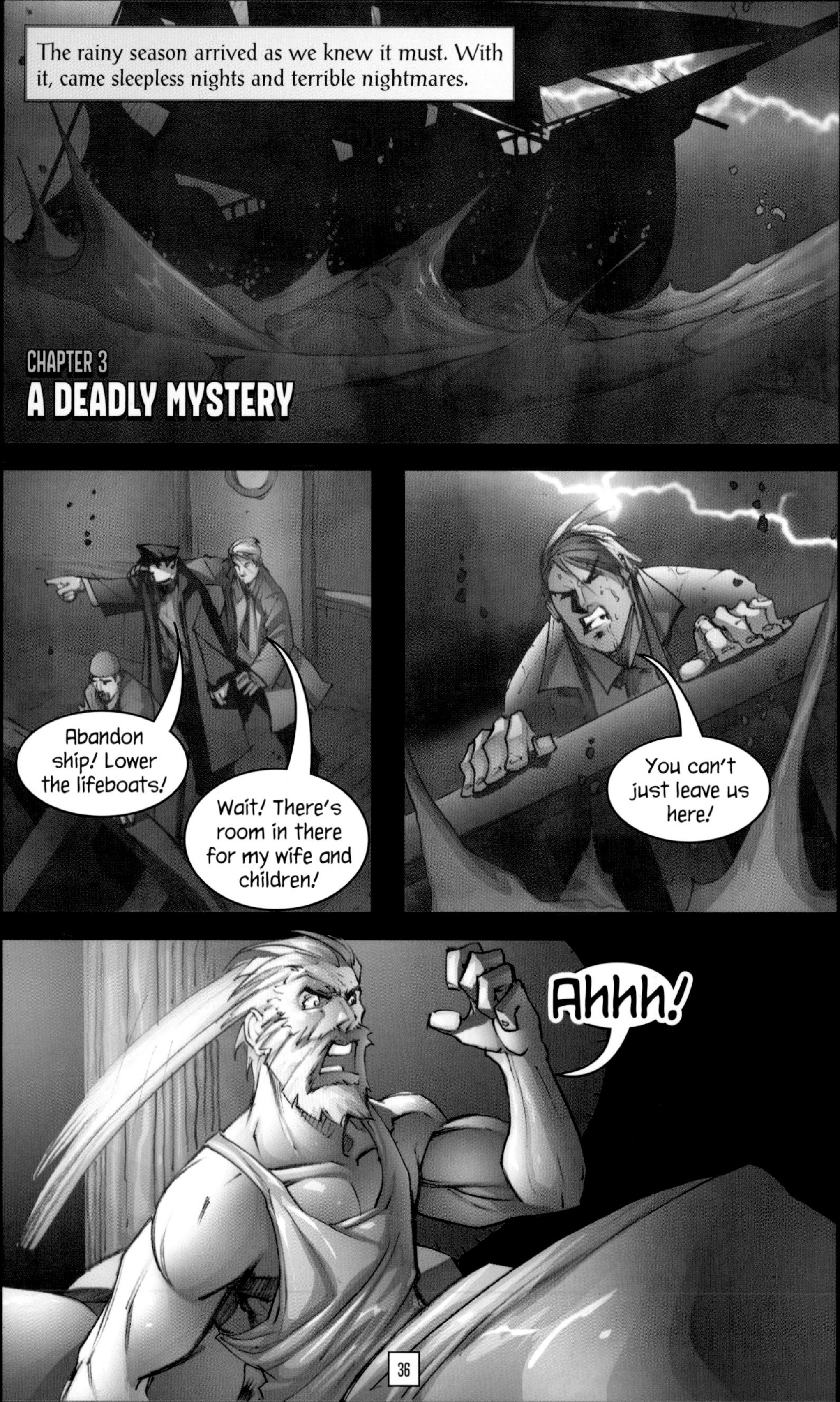
The rainy season arrived as we knew it must. With it, came sleepless nights and terrible nightmares.
CHAPTER 3
A DEADLY MYSTERY
Abandon ship! Lower the lifeboats!
Wait! There's room in there for my wife and children!
You can't just leave us here!
Ahhh!

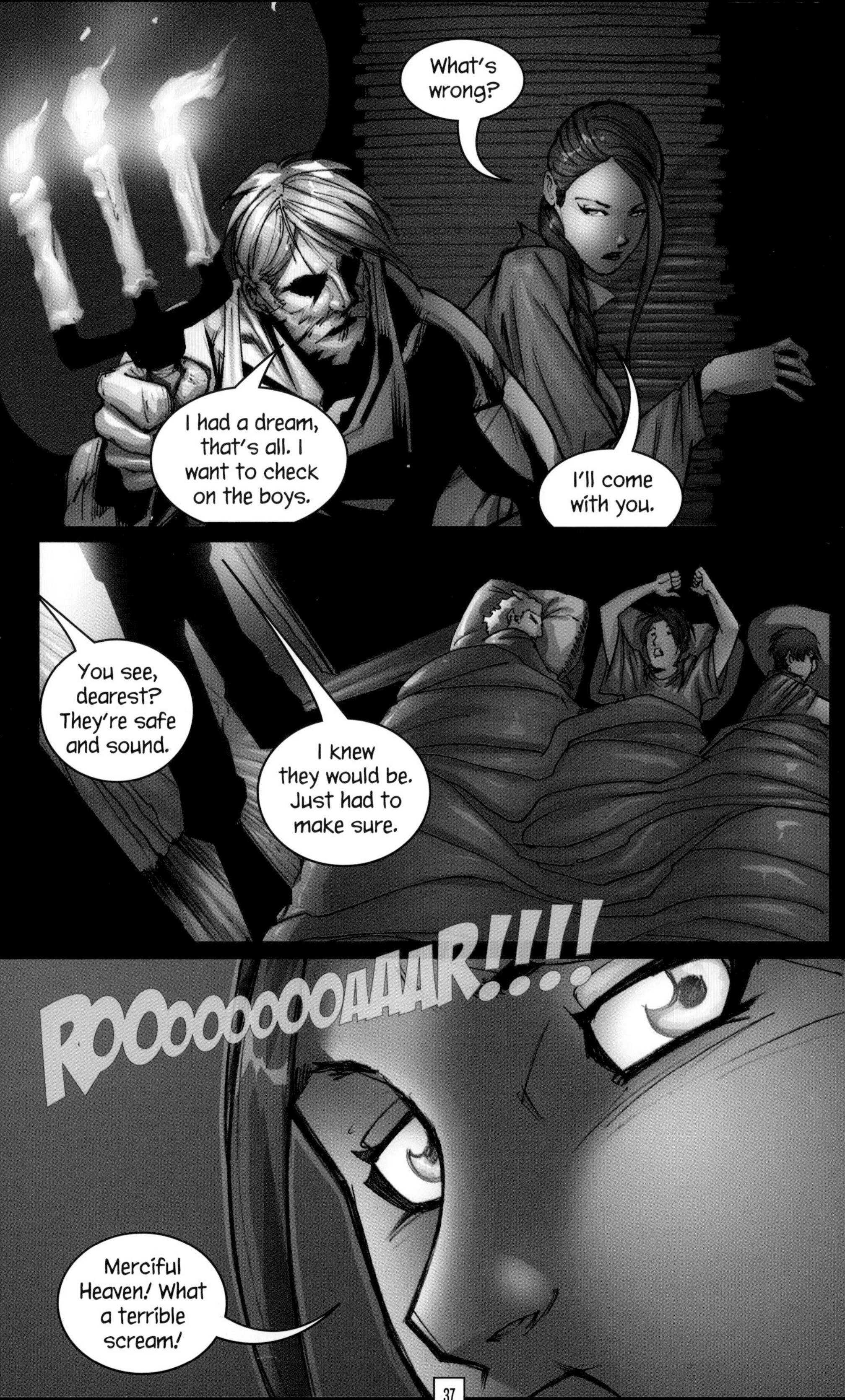
What's wrong?
I had a dream, that's all. I want to check on the boys.
I'll come with you.
You see, dearest? They're safe and sound.
I knew they would be. Just had to make sure.
ROOOOOOOOAAAR!!!!
Merciful Heaven! What a terrible scream!

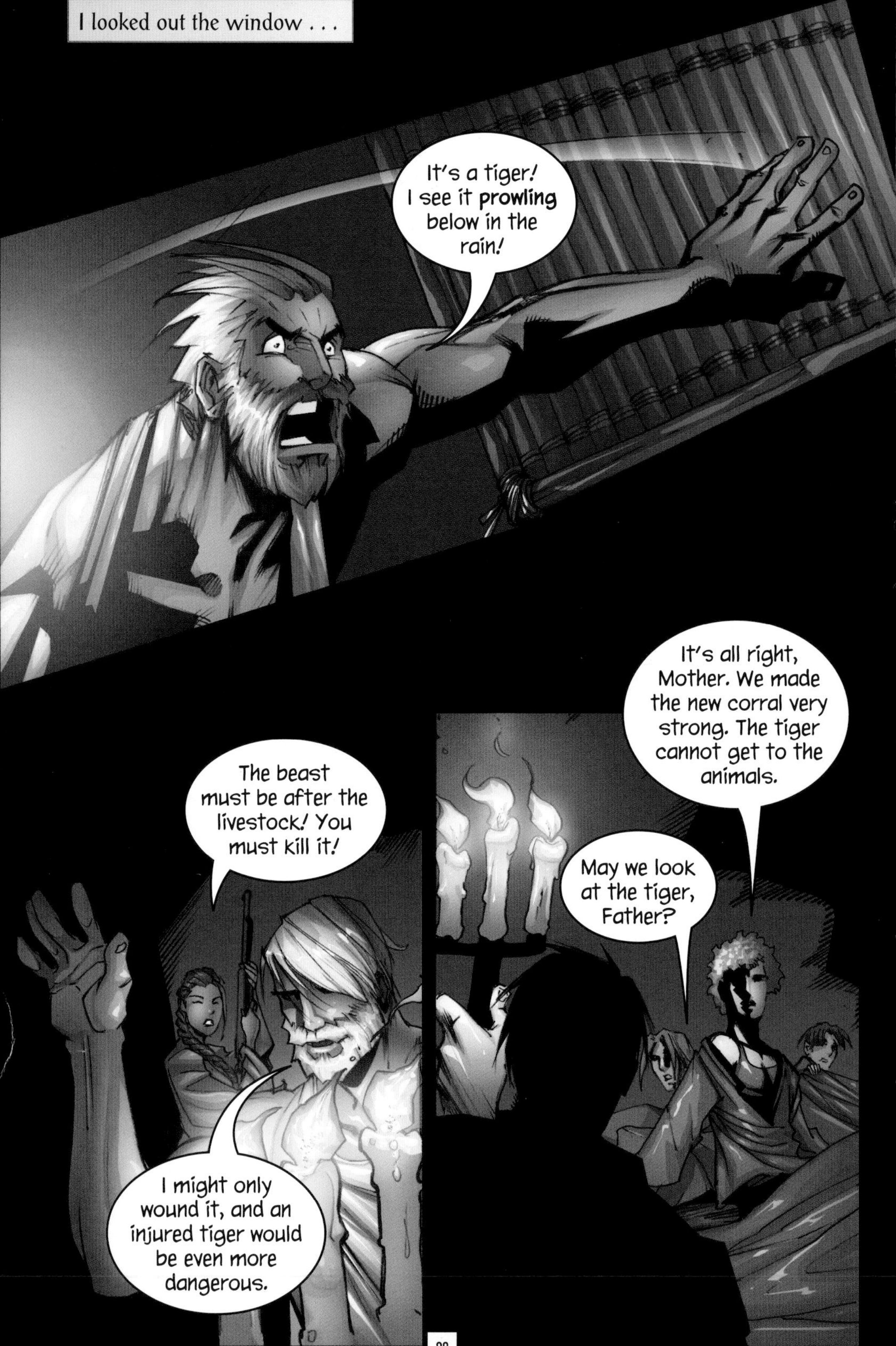
I looked out the window . . .
It's a tiger! I see it prowling below in the rain!
The beast must be after the livestock! You must kill it!
I might only wound it, and an injured tiger would be even more dangerous.
It's all right, Mother. We made the new corral very strong. The tiger cannot get to the animals.
May we look at the tiger, Father?

You'll see him soon enough. It's back to bed for all of us. Let's get what rest we can.
There's a tiger to hunt in the morning.
ROOOOOOOOAAAR!!!!

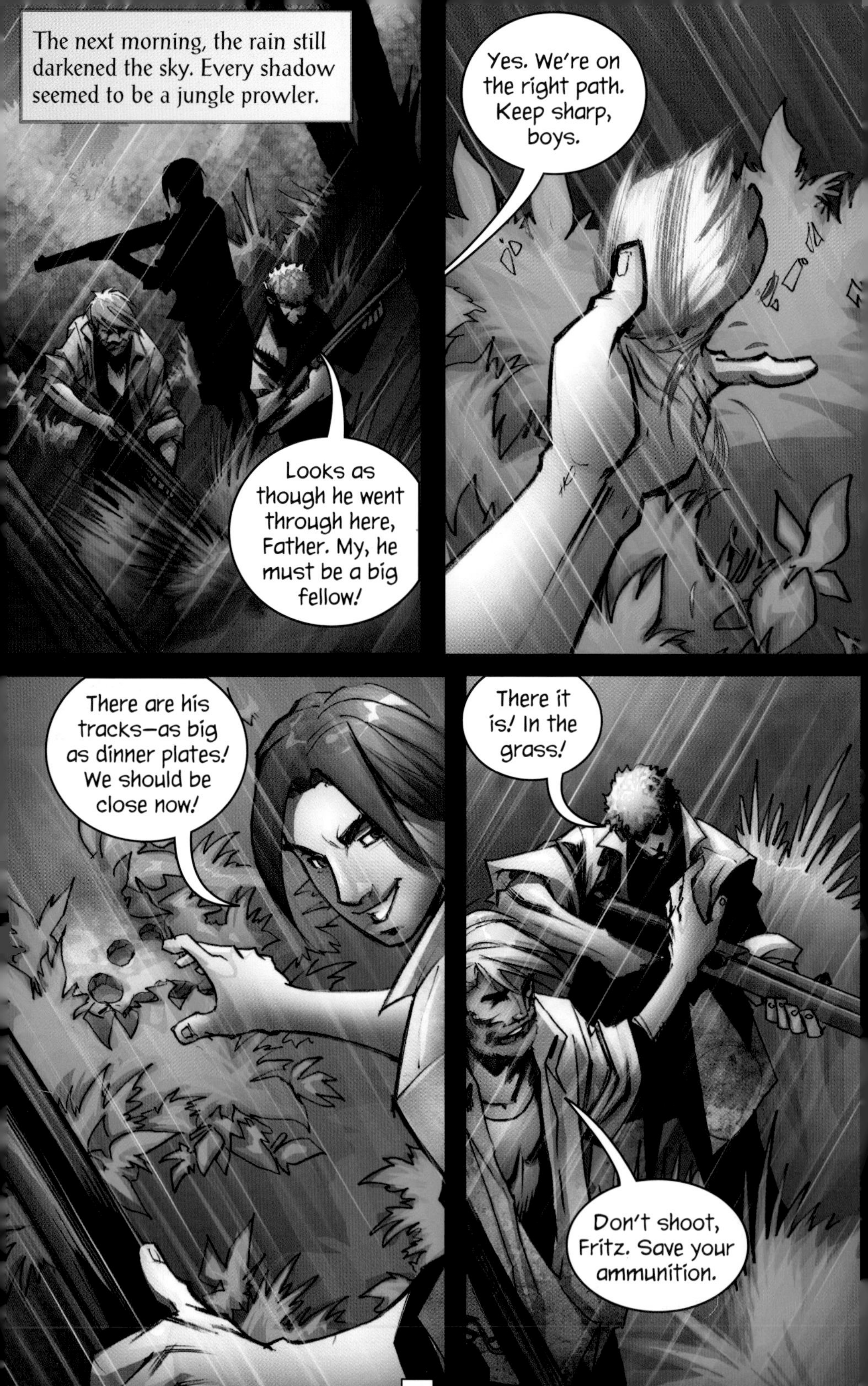

The next morning, the rain still darkened the sky. Every shadow seemed to be a jungle prowler.
Looks as though he went through here, Father. My, he must be a big fellow!
Yes. We're on the right path. Keep sharp, boys.
There are his tracks—as big as dinner plates! We should be close now!
There it is! In the grass!
Don't shoot, Fritz. Save your ammunition.

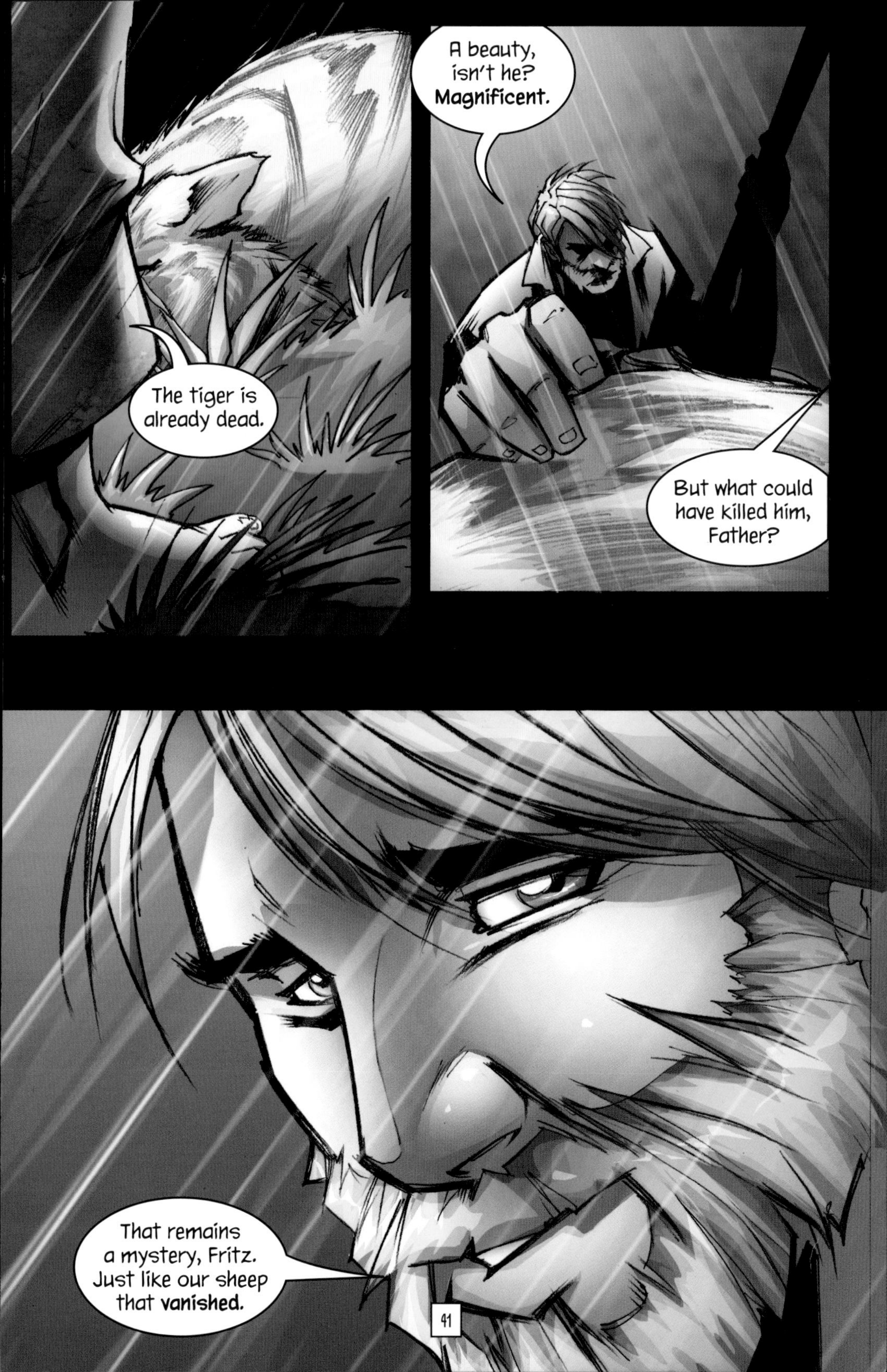
The tiger is already dead.
A beauty, isn't he? Magnificent.
But what could have killed him, Father?
That remains a mystery, Fritz. Just like our sheep that vanished.

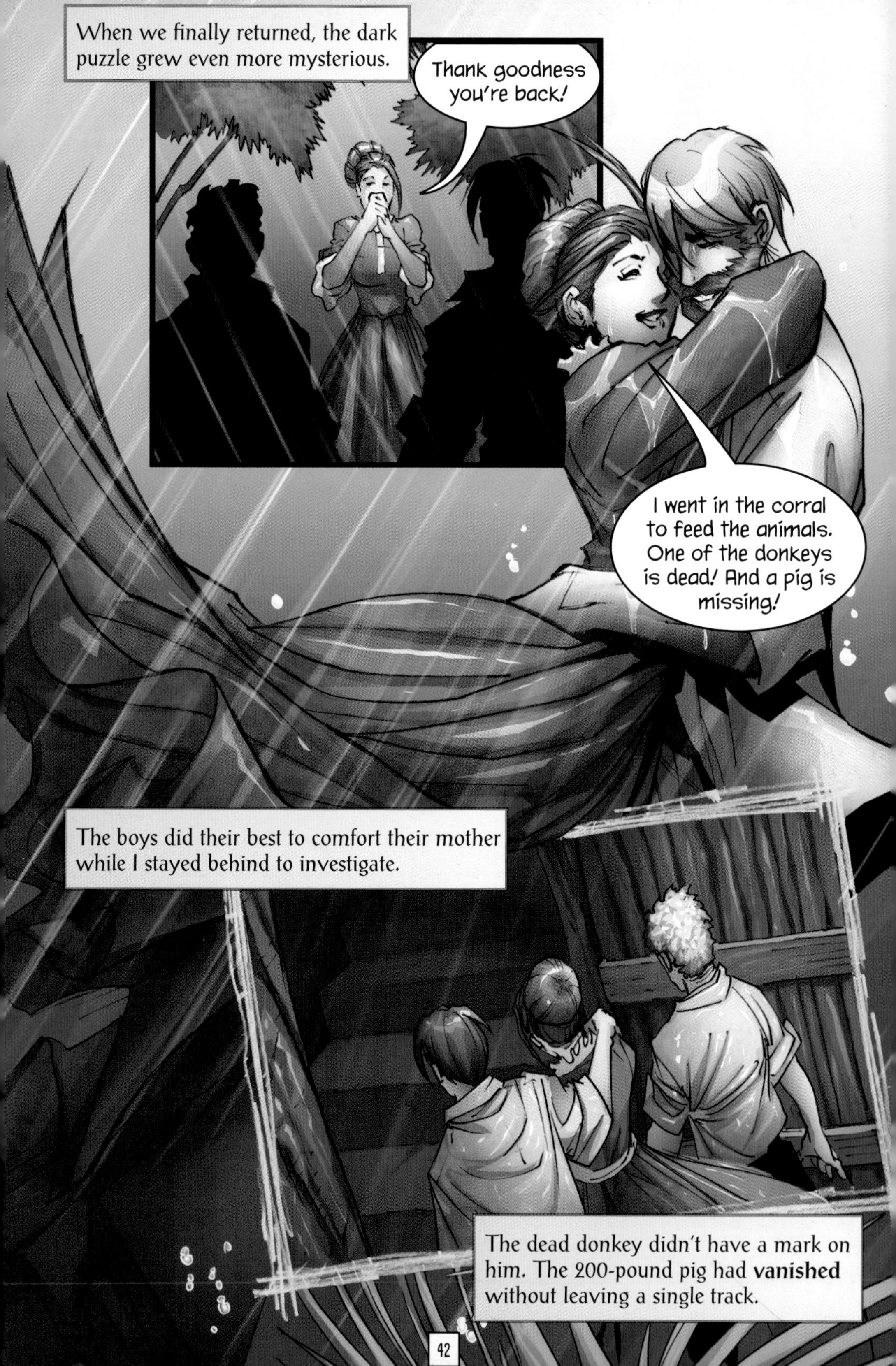

When we finally returned, the dark puzzle grew even more mysterious.
Thank goodness you're back!
I went in the corral to feed the animals. One of the donkeys is dead! And a pig is missing!
The boys did their best to comfort their mother while I stayed behind to investigate.
The dead donkey didn't have a mark on him. The 200-pound pig had **vanished** without leaving a single track.

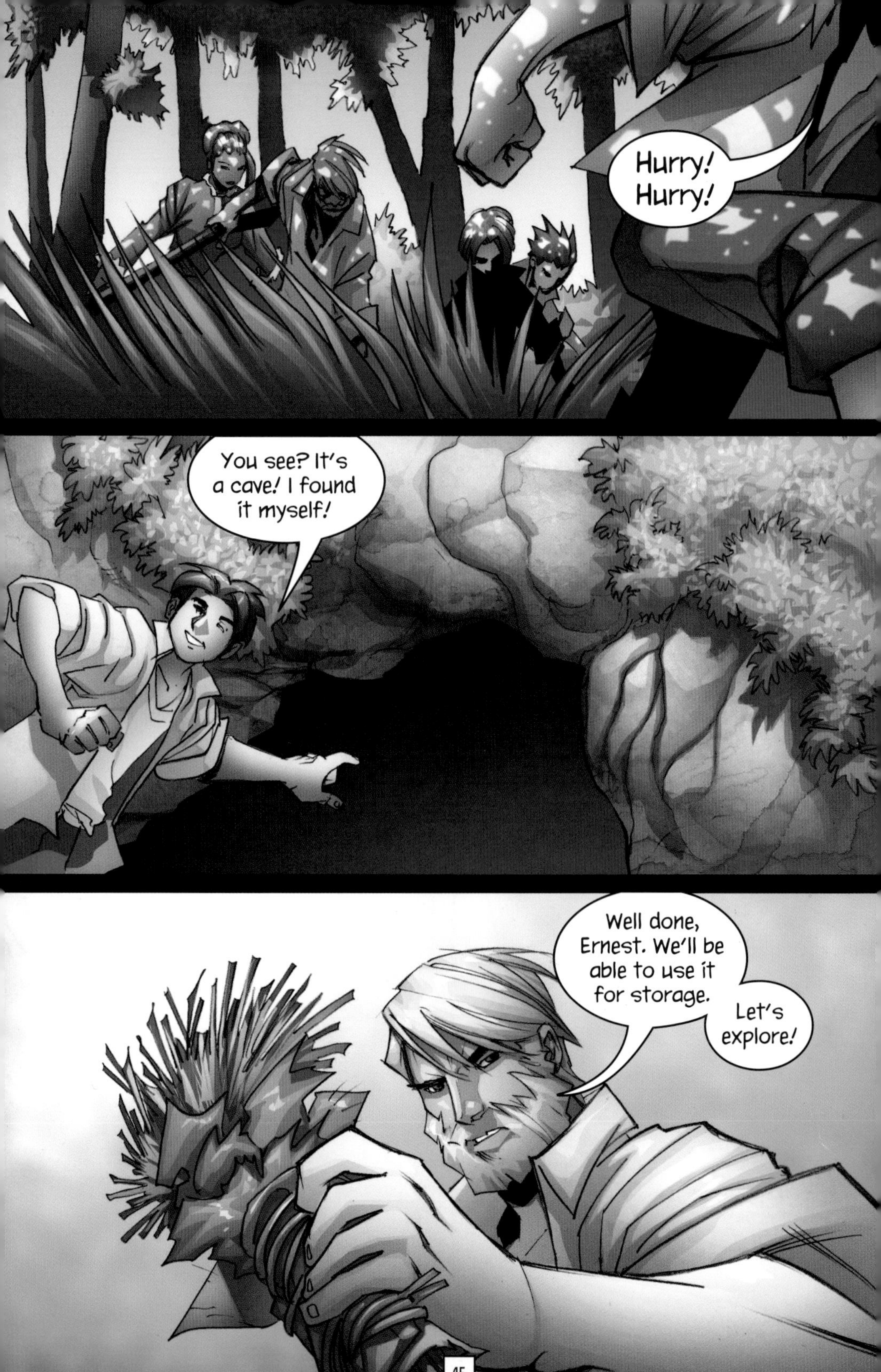
Hurry! Hurry!
You see? It's a cave! I found it myself!
Well done, Ernest. We'll be able to use it for storage.
Let's explore!

A cave of rock salt.
It must have been carved by this stream, which was once a mighty river long, long ago.
It's perfect. This will be our new winter home!

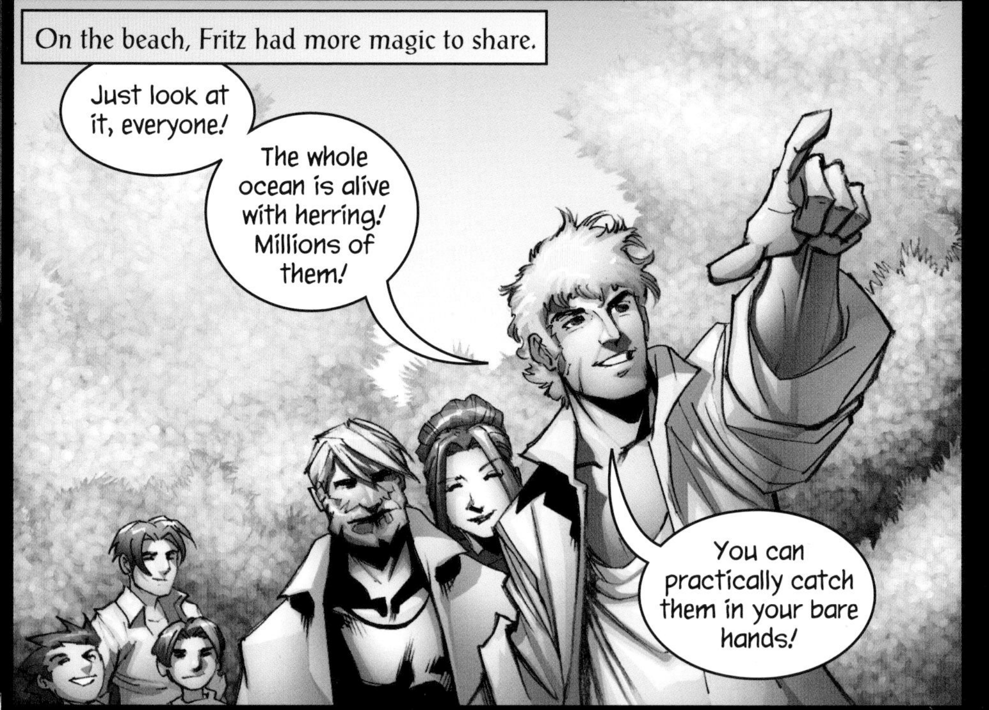
On the beach, Fritz had more magic to share.
Just look at it, everyone!
The whole ocean is alive with herring! Millions of them!
You can practically catch them in your bare hands!

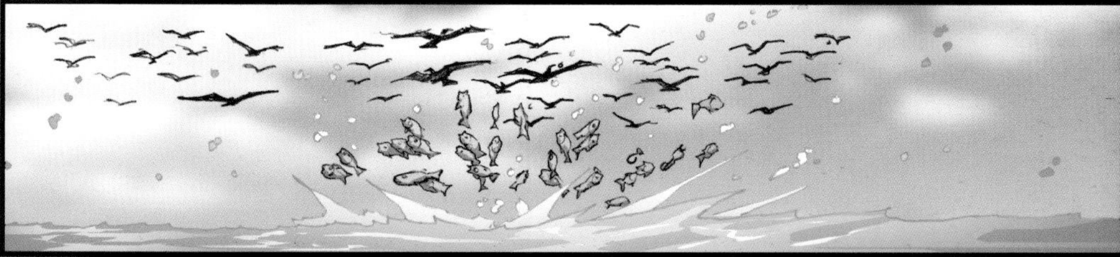

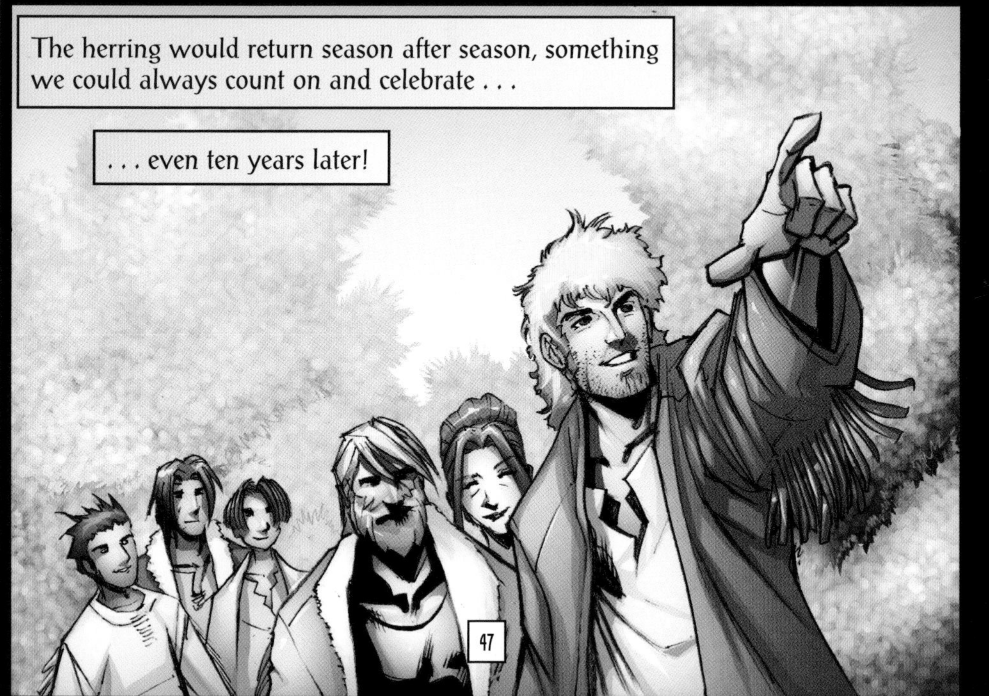
The herring would return season after season, something we could always count on and celebrate . . .
. . . even ten years later!

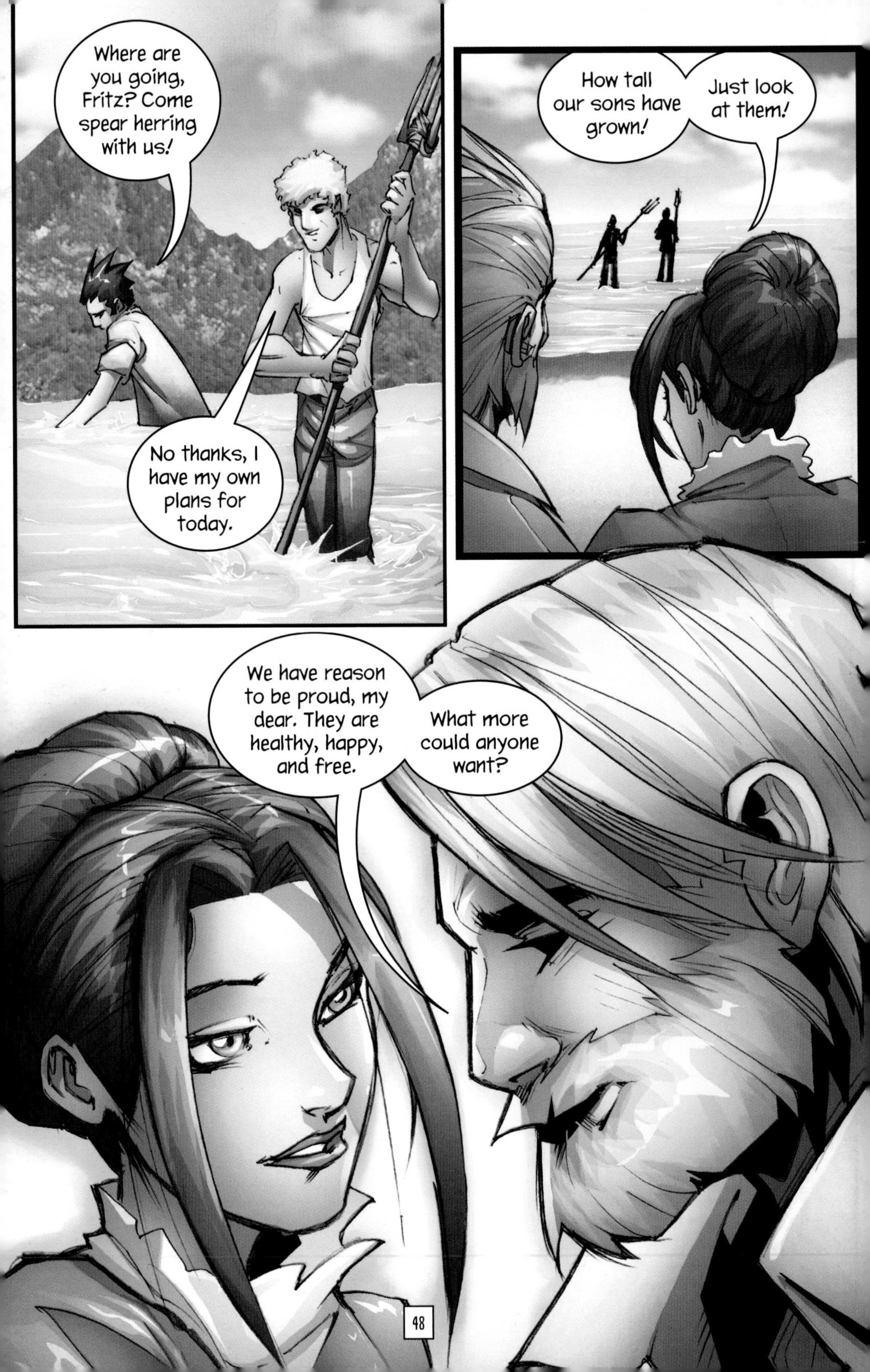

Where are you going, Fritz? Come spear herring with us!
No thanks, I have my own plans for today.
How tall our sons have grown!
Just look at them!
We have reason to be proud, my dear. They are healthy, happy, and free.
What more could anyone want?

CHAPTER 5
FRITZ'S DISCOVERY

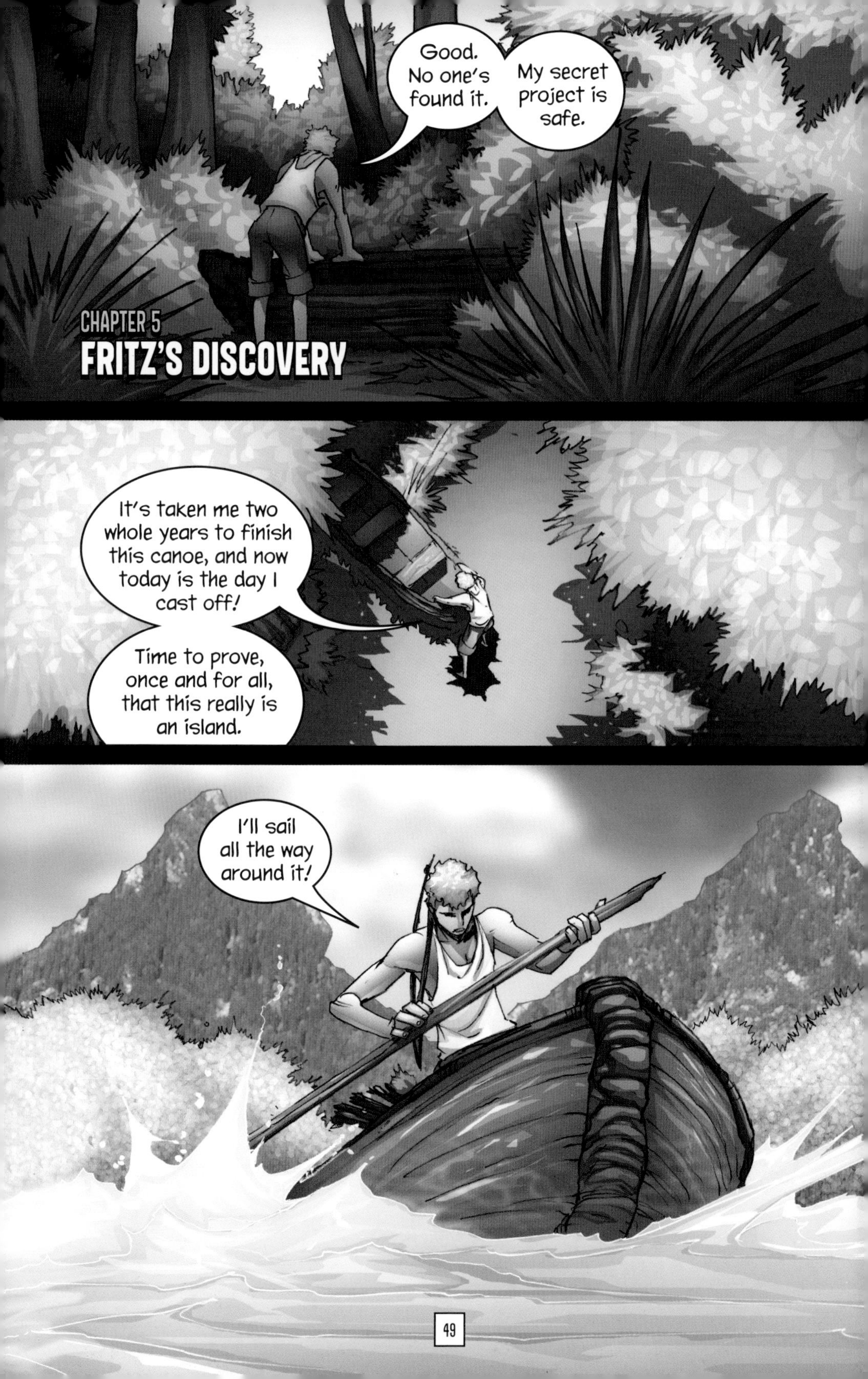
Good. No one's found it.
My secret project is safe.
It's taken me two whole years to finish this canoe, and now today is the day I cast off!
Time to prove, once and for all, that this really is an island.
I'll sail all the way around it!

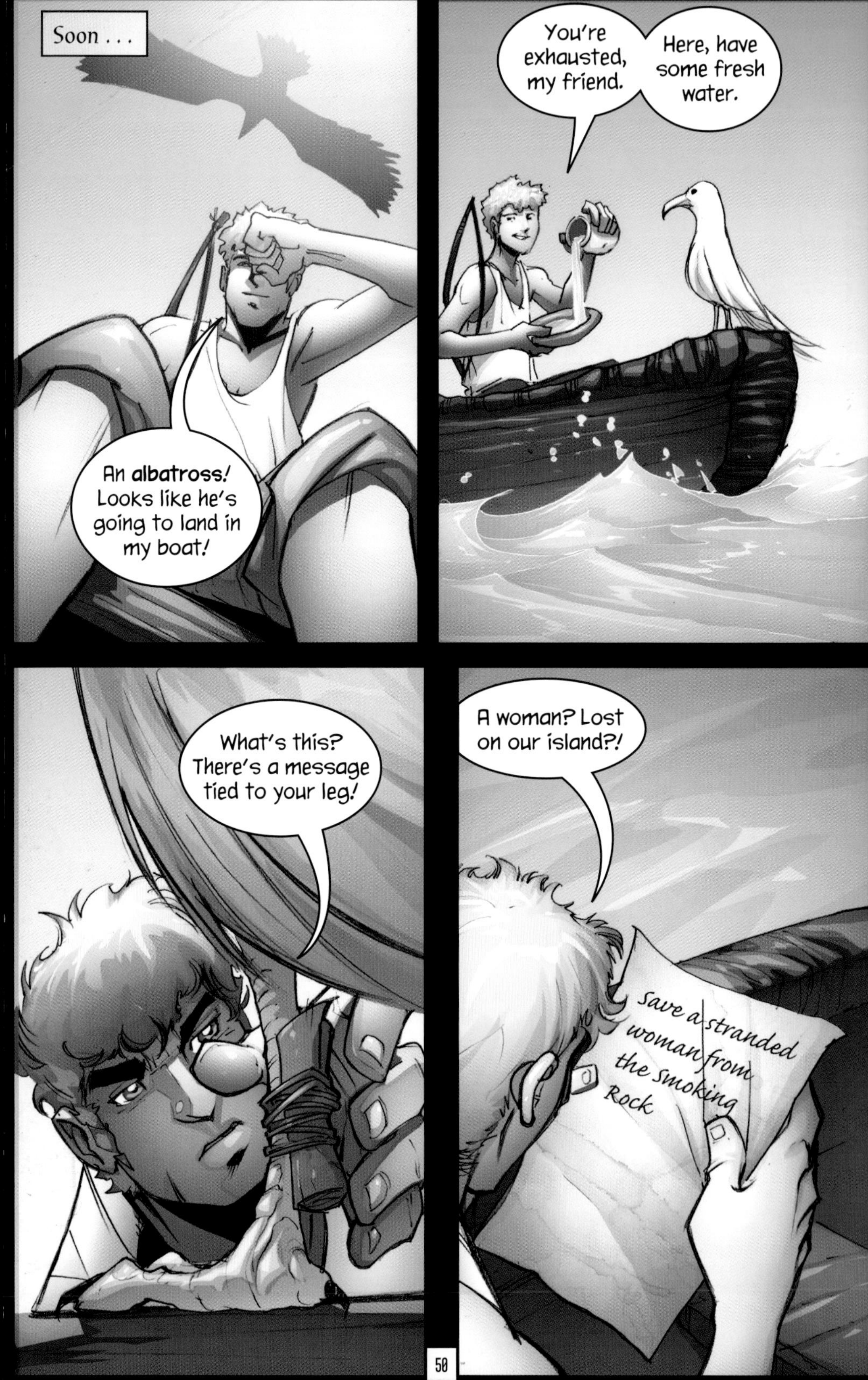
Soon . . .
An **albatross!** Looks like he's going to land in my boat!
You're exhausted, my friend.
Here, have some fresh water.
What's this? There's a message tied to your leg!
A woman? Lost on our island?!
Save a stranded woman from the Smoking Rock

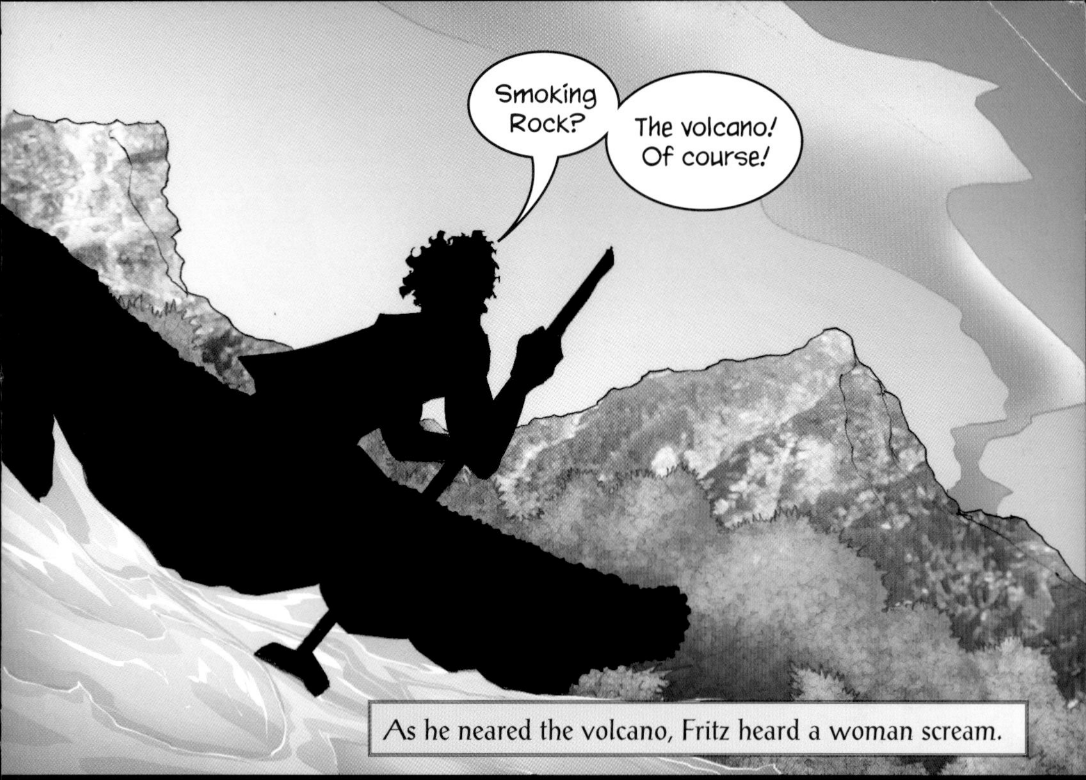
Smoking Rock?
The volcano! Of course!
As he neared the volcano, Fritz heard a woman scream.

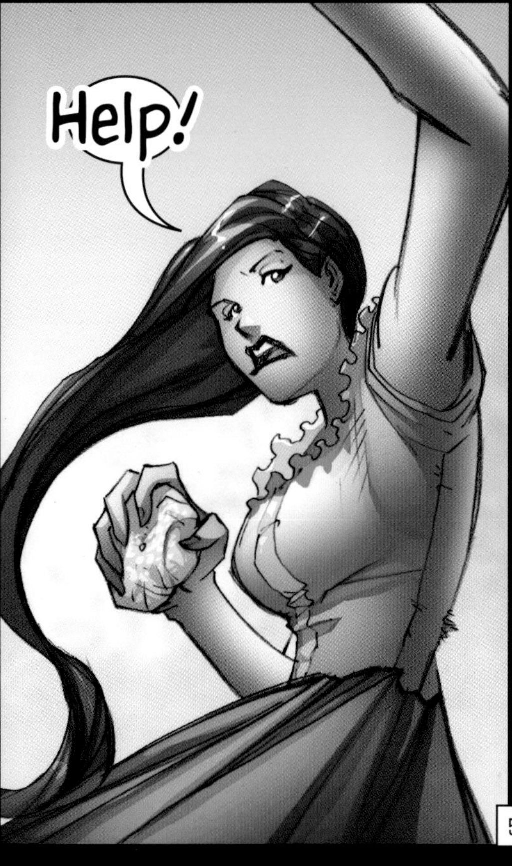
Help!

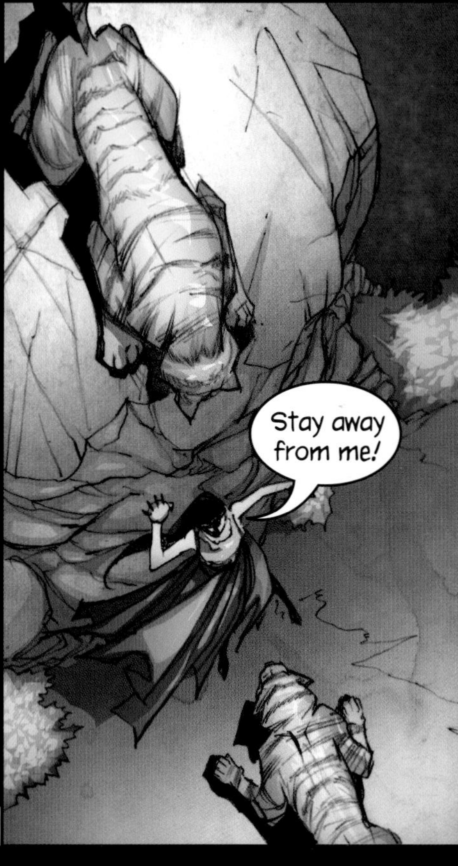
Stay away from me!

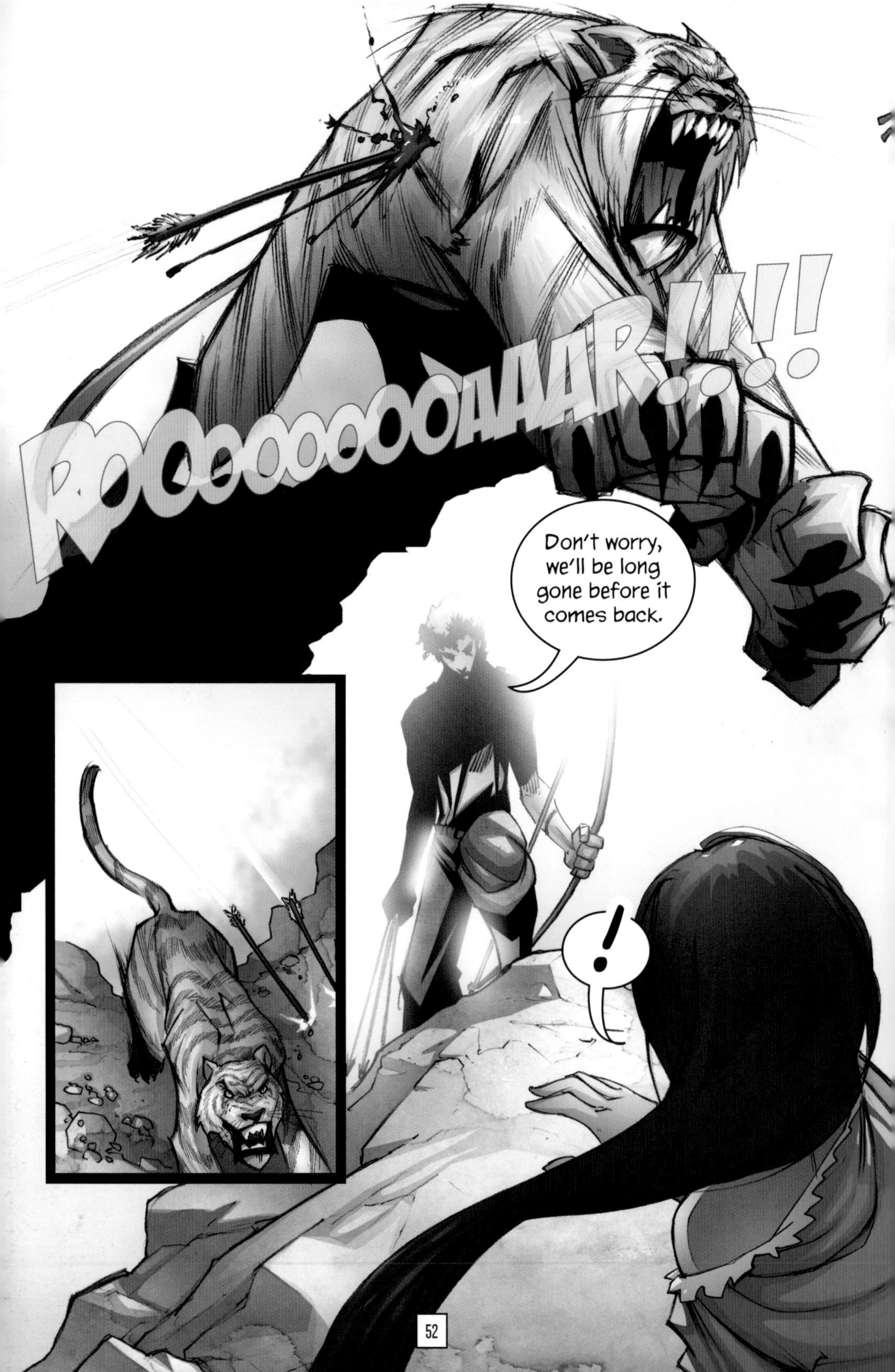
ROOOOOOOOAAAR!!!!!
Don't worry, we'll be long gone before it comes back.
!

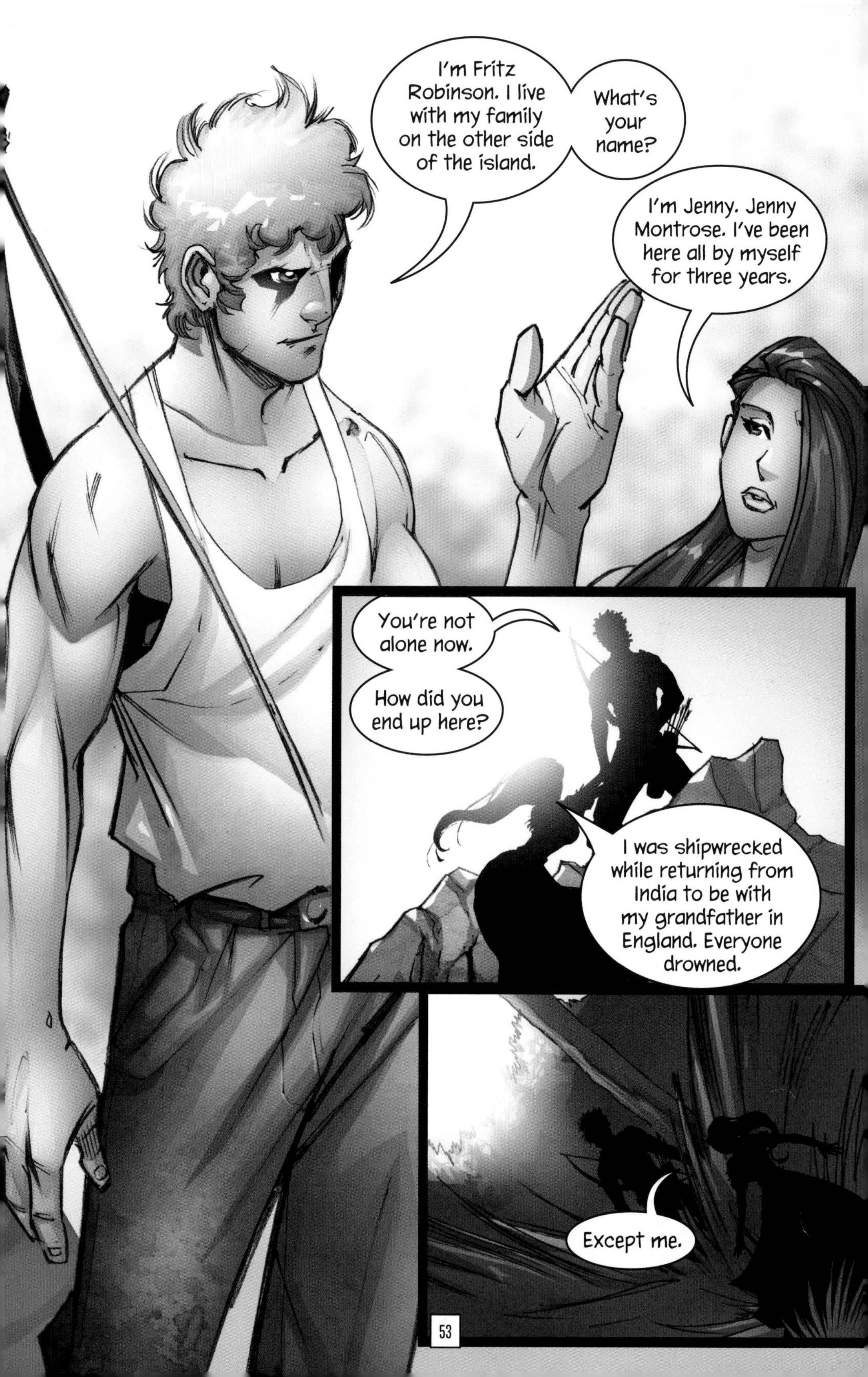
I'm Fritz Robinson. I live with my family on the other side of the island.
What's your name?
I'm Jenny. Jenny Montrose. I've been here all by myself for three years.
You're not alone now.
How did you end up here?
I was shipwrecked while returning from India to be with my grandfather in England. Everyone drowned.
Except me.

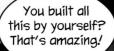

You built all this by yourself? That's amazing!

It's nice, but I want to be with other people again.

Don't worry, you'll fit right in. My mother always wanted a daughter.

A short time later . . .

Your home! It's even more beautiful than you described!

Yes, but something is wrong.

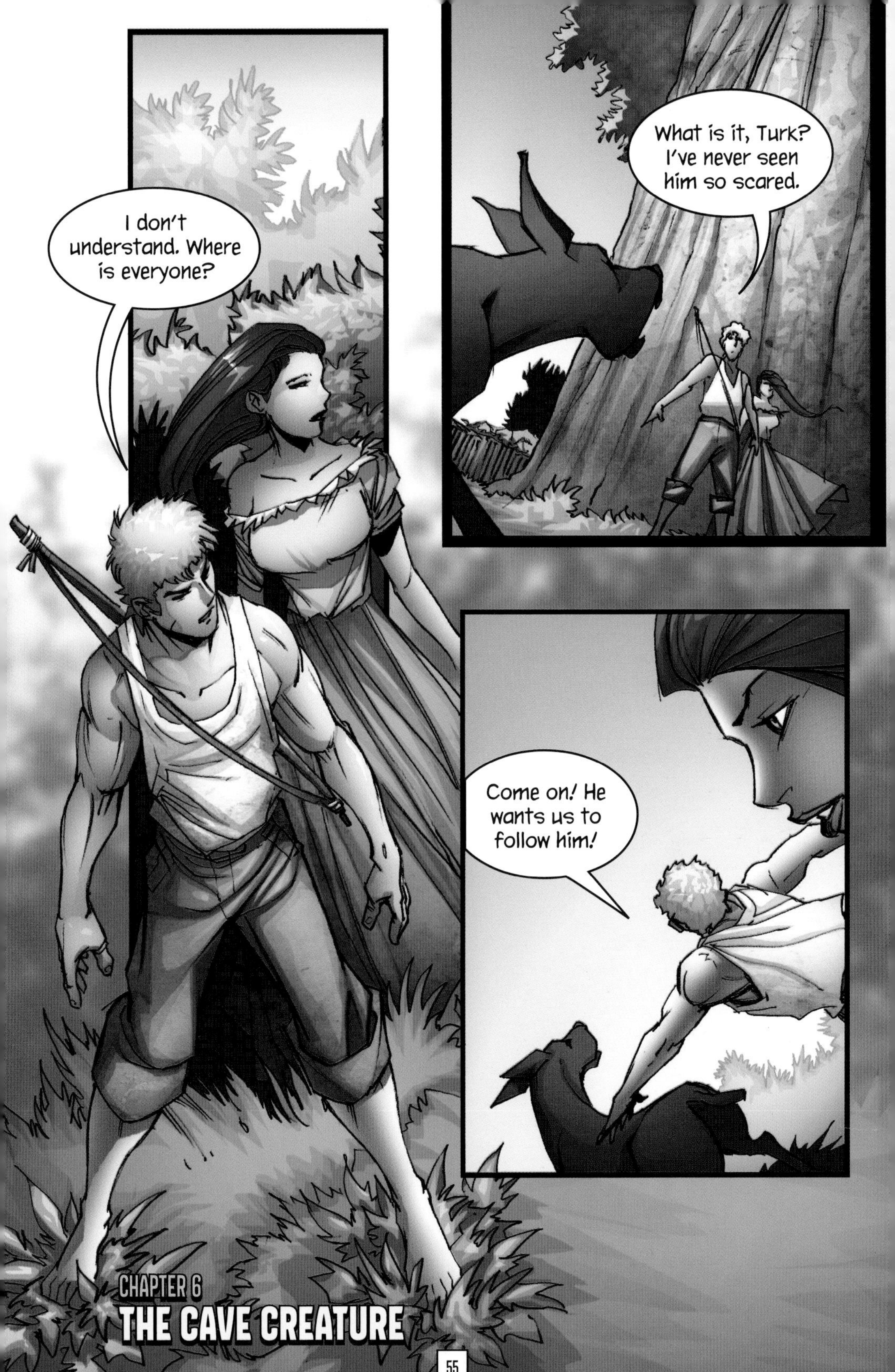
I don't understand. Where is everyone?
What is it, Turk? I've never seen him so scared.
Come on! He wants us to follow him!
CHAPTER 6
THE CAVE CREATURE

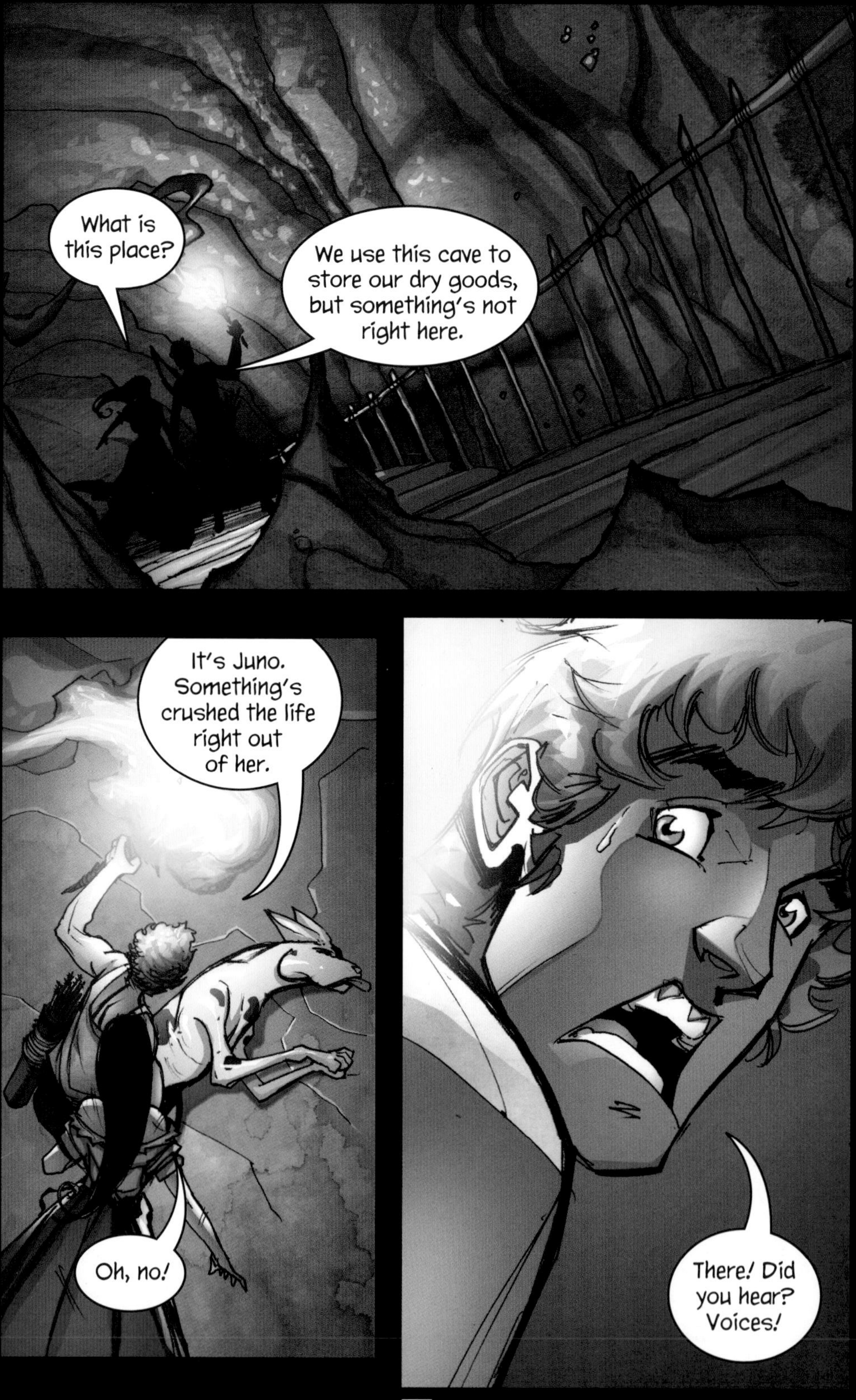
What is this place?
We use this cave to store our dry goods, but something's not right here.
It's Juno. Something's crushed the life right out of her.
Oh, no!
There! Did you hear? Voices!

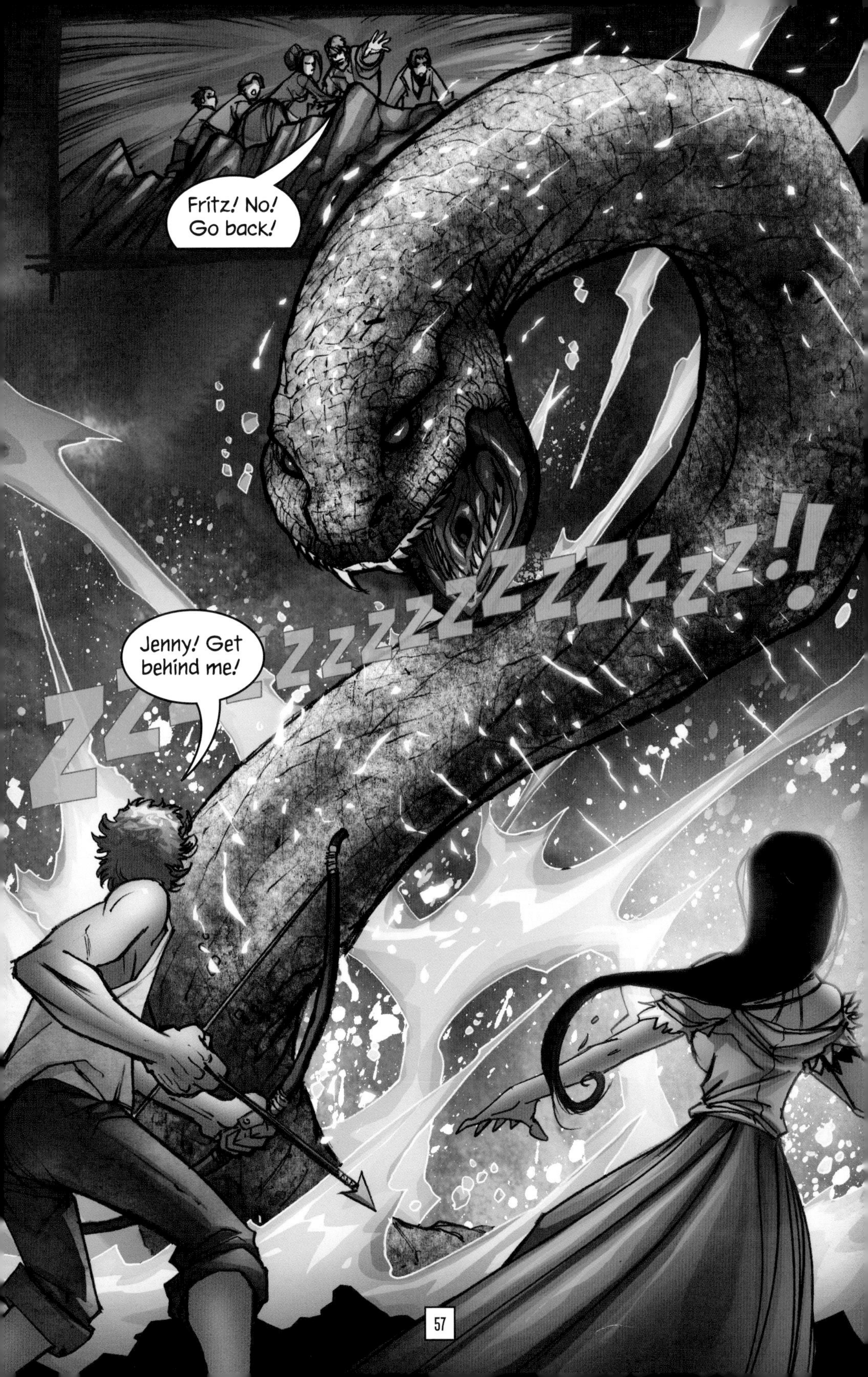
Fritz! No! Go back!
ZZZZZZZZZZZZZZZZ!!
Jenny! Get behind me!

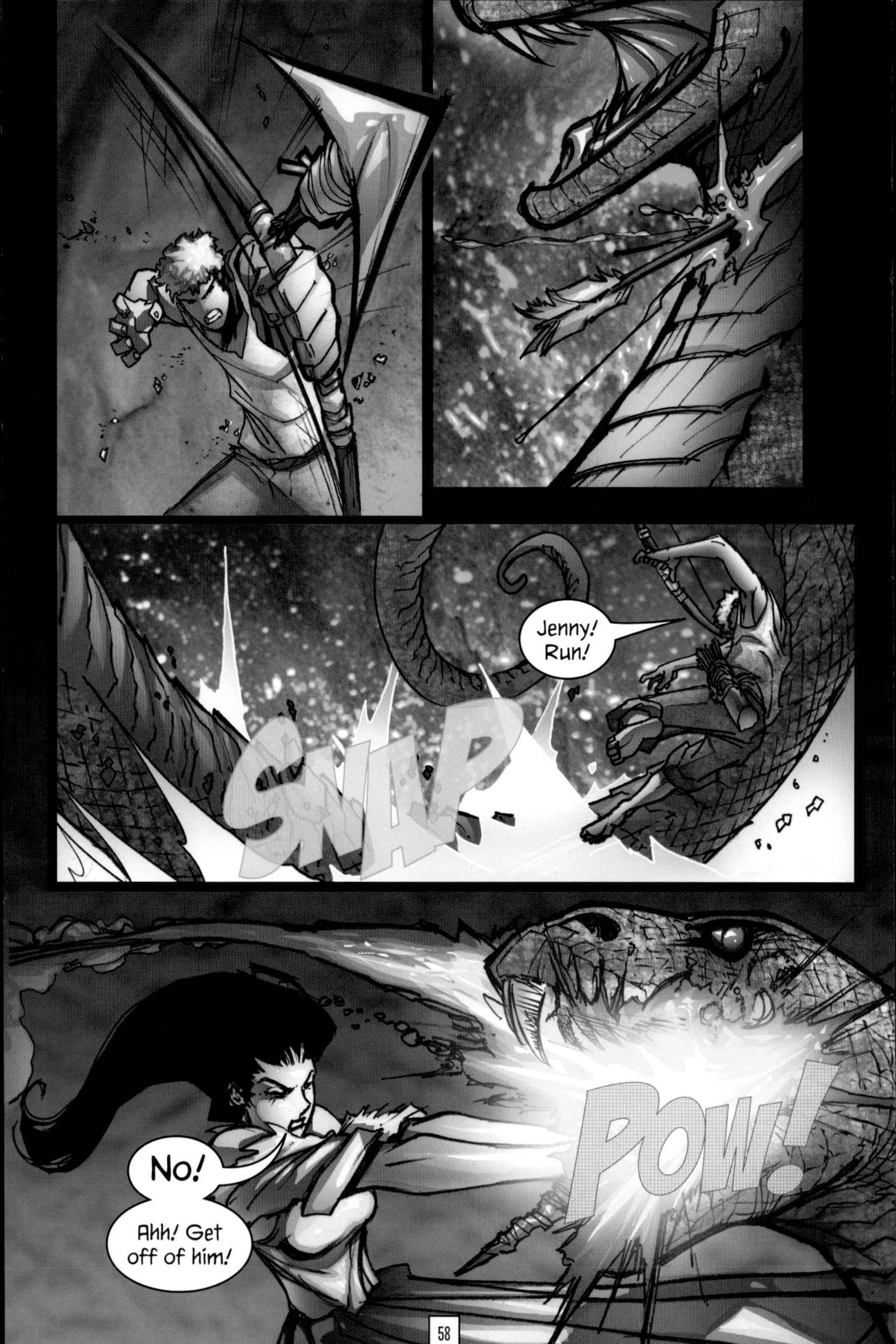
Jenny! Run!
SNAP
No!
Ahh! Get off of him!
POW!

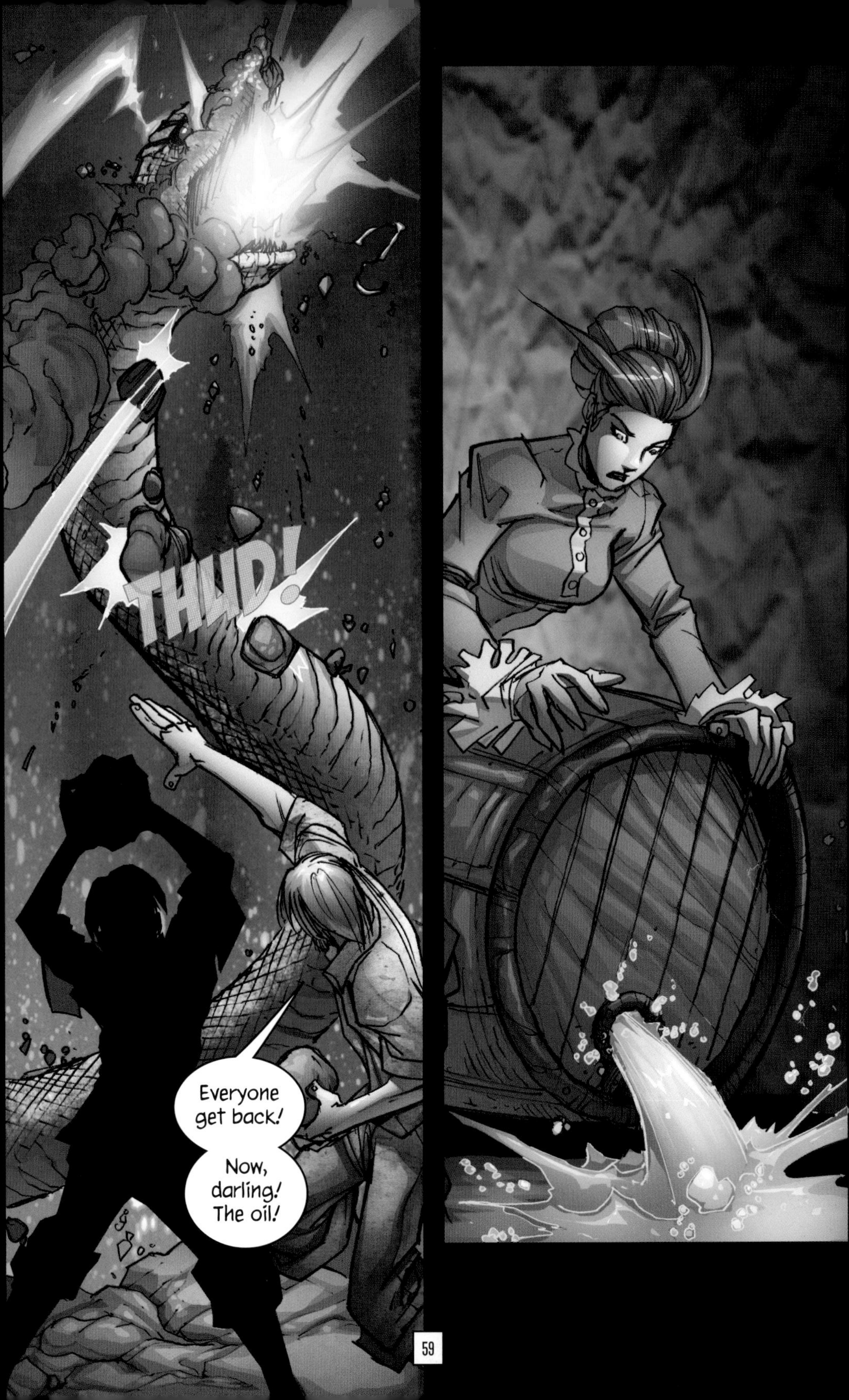
THUD!
Everyone get back!
Now, darling! The oil!

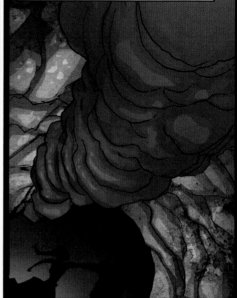

Suddenly a dozen dark mysteries were made clear. Now the monster was destroyed.

Our nameless horror, at long last, had a form. It was a gigantic boa constrictor, over forty feet in length.

We took Jenny instantly to our hearts. She was braver than any we'd ever known. Now, she had a new family.

And she and Fritz had each other.

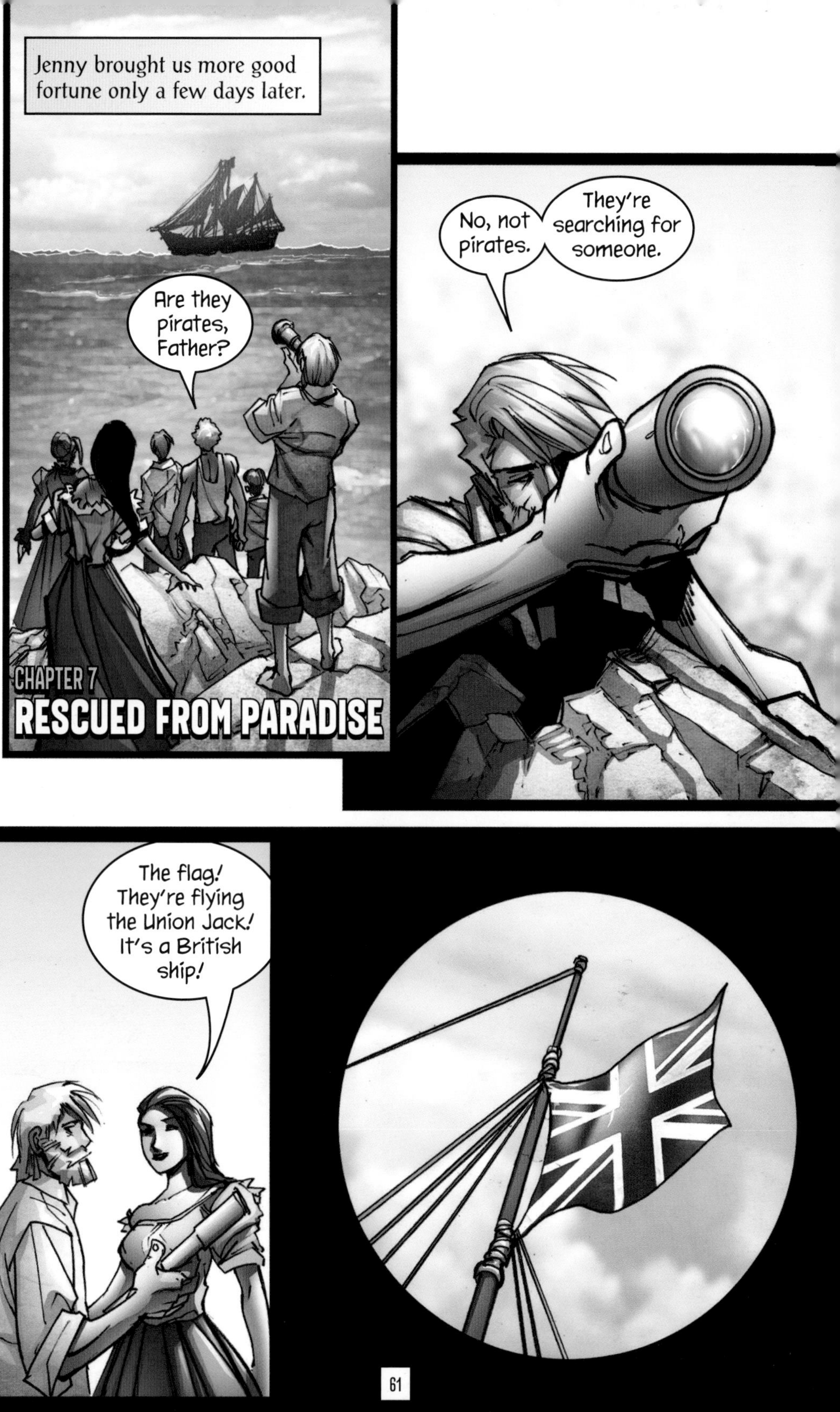
Jenny brought us more good fortune only a few days later.
Are they pirates, Father?
CHAPTER 7
RESCUED FROM PARADISE
No, not pirates.
They're searching for someone.
The flag! They're flying the Union Jack! It's a British ship!

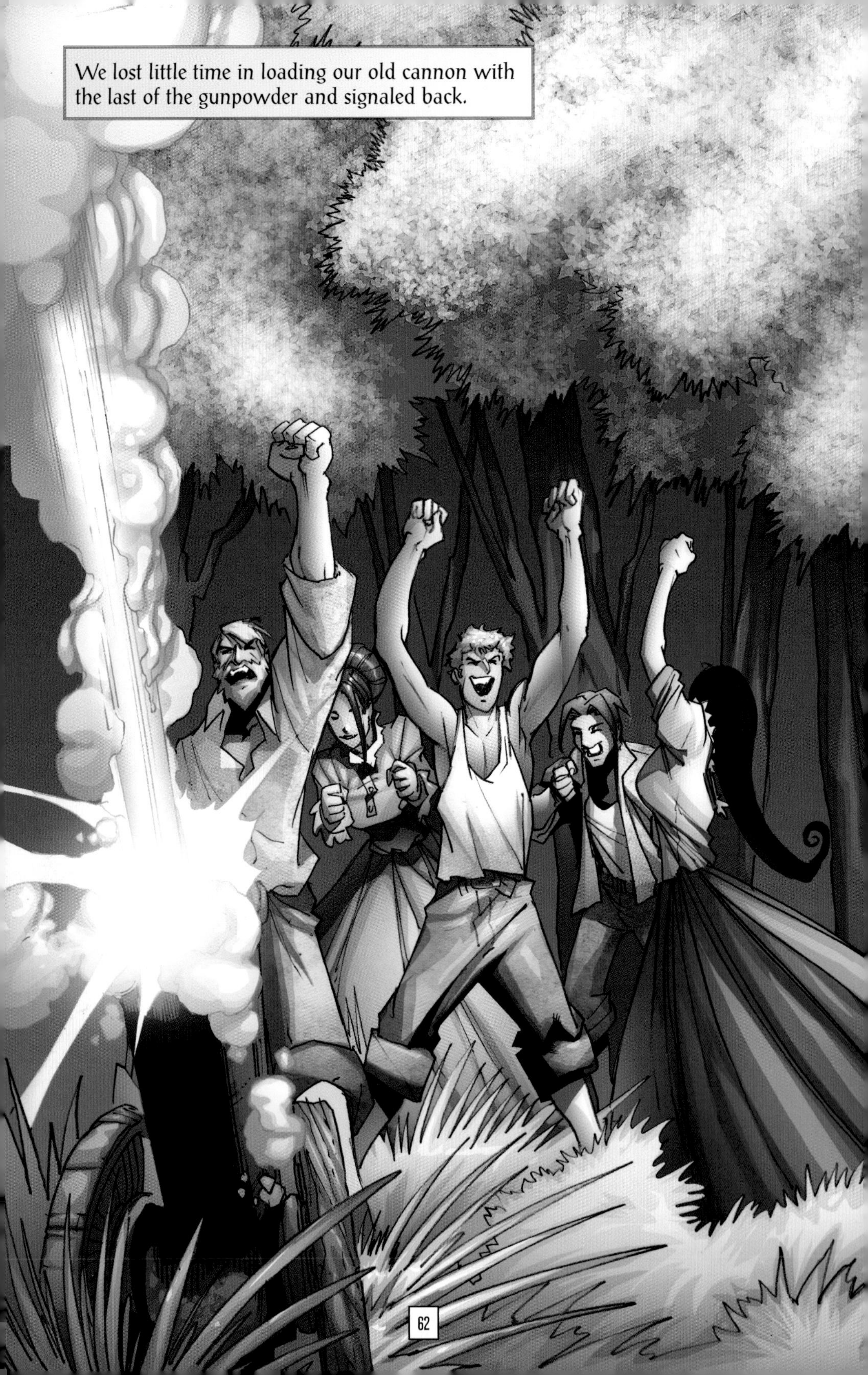
We lost little time in loading our old cannon with the last of the gunpowder and signaled back.

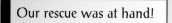
Our rescue was at hand!

Welcome, Captain. I'm Jenny Montrose.

Saints be praised! Your grandfather has had us searching the Seven Seas for you, girl!

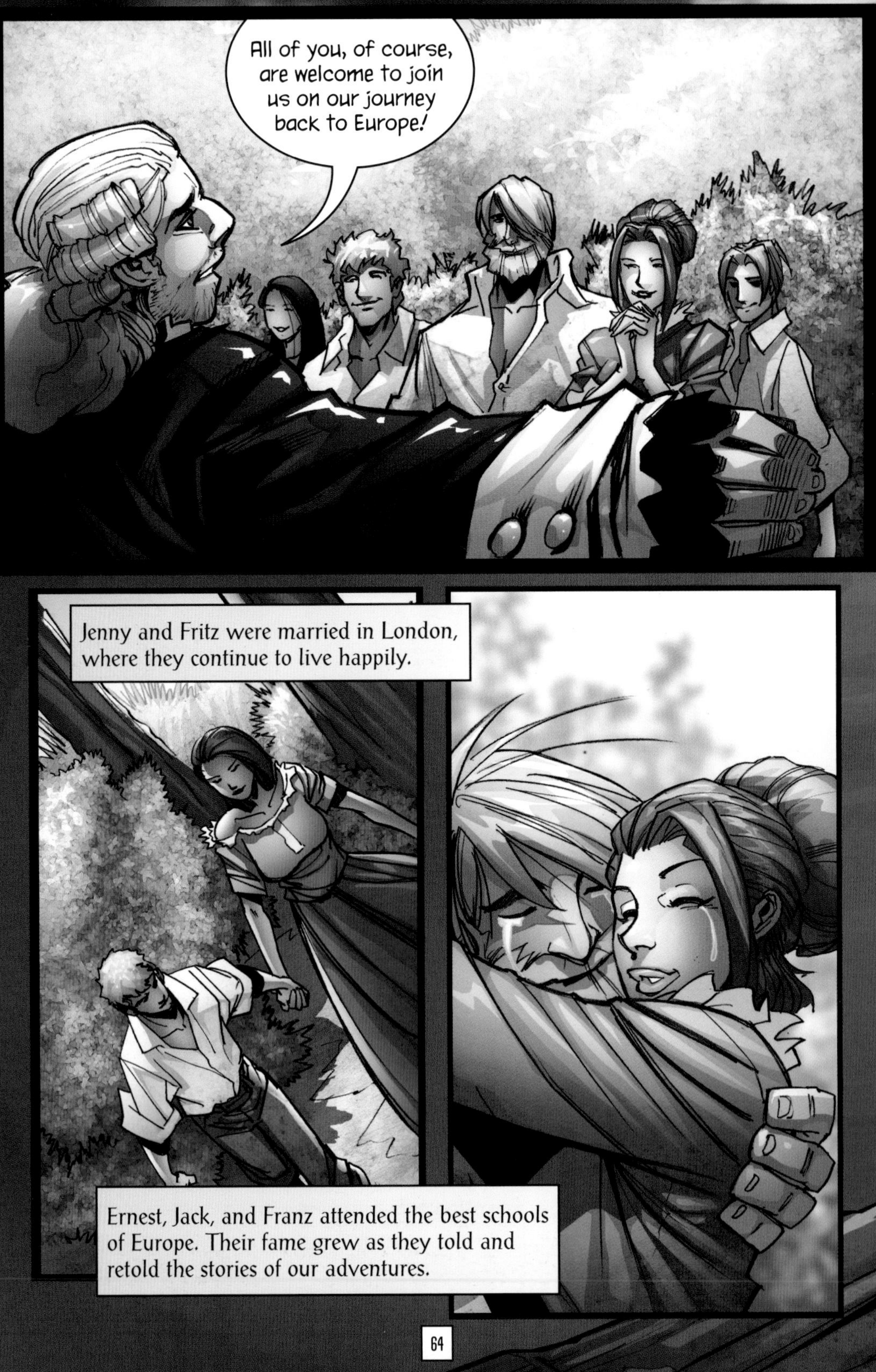
All of you, of course, are welcome to join us on our journey back to Europe!
Jenny and Fritz were married in London, where they continue to live happily.
Ernest, Jack, and Franz attended the best schools of Europe. Their fame grew as they told and retold the stories of our adventures.

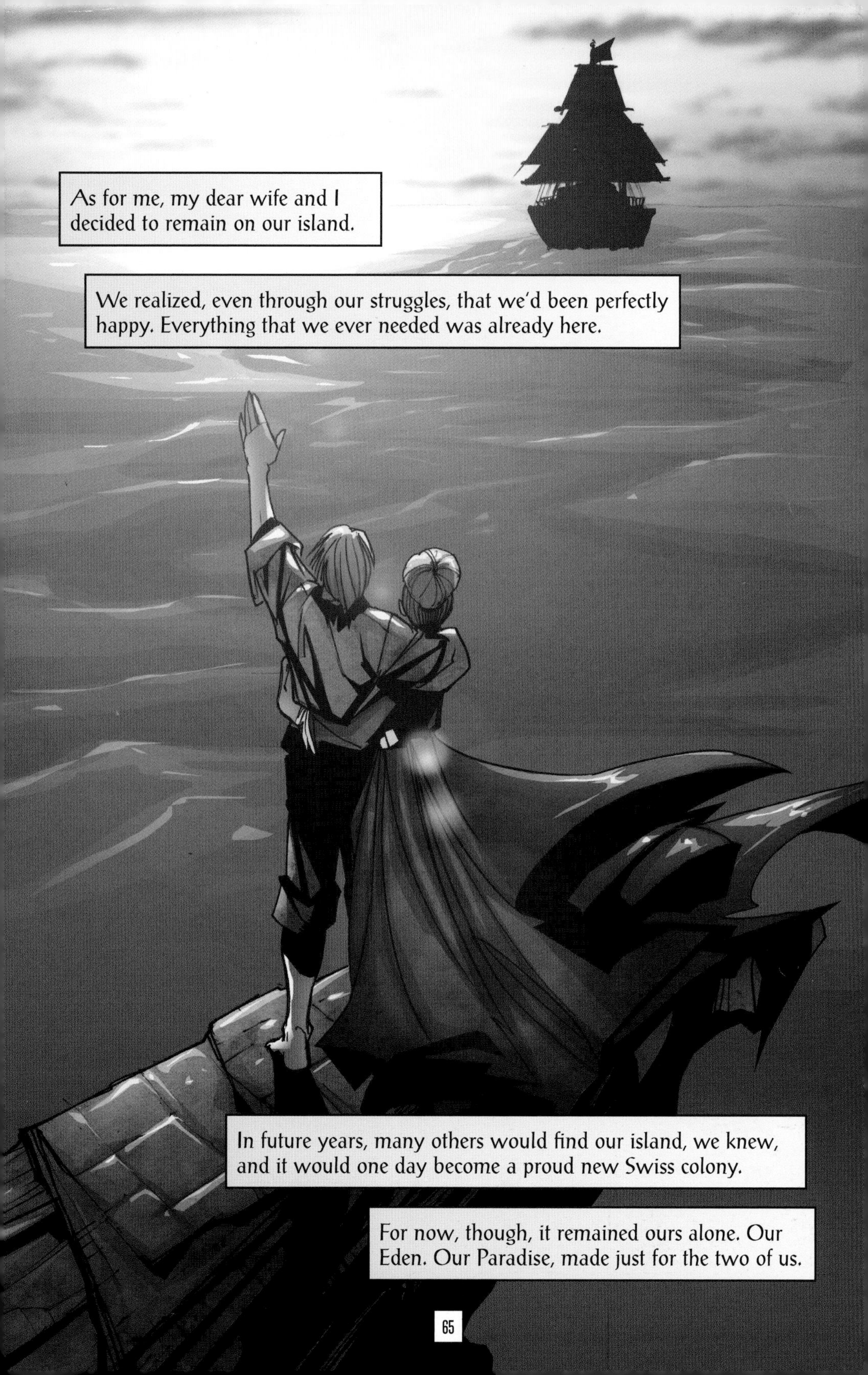
As for me, my dear wife and I decided to remain on our island.
We realized, even through our struggles, that we'd been perfectly happy. Everything that we ever needed was already here.
In future years, many others would find our island, we knew, and it would one day become a proud new Swiss colony.
For now, though, it remained ours alone. Our Eden. Our Paradise, made just for the two of us.

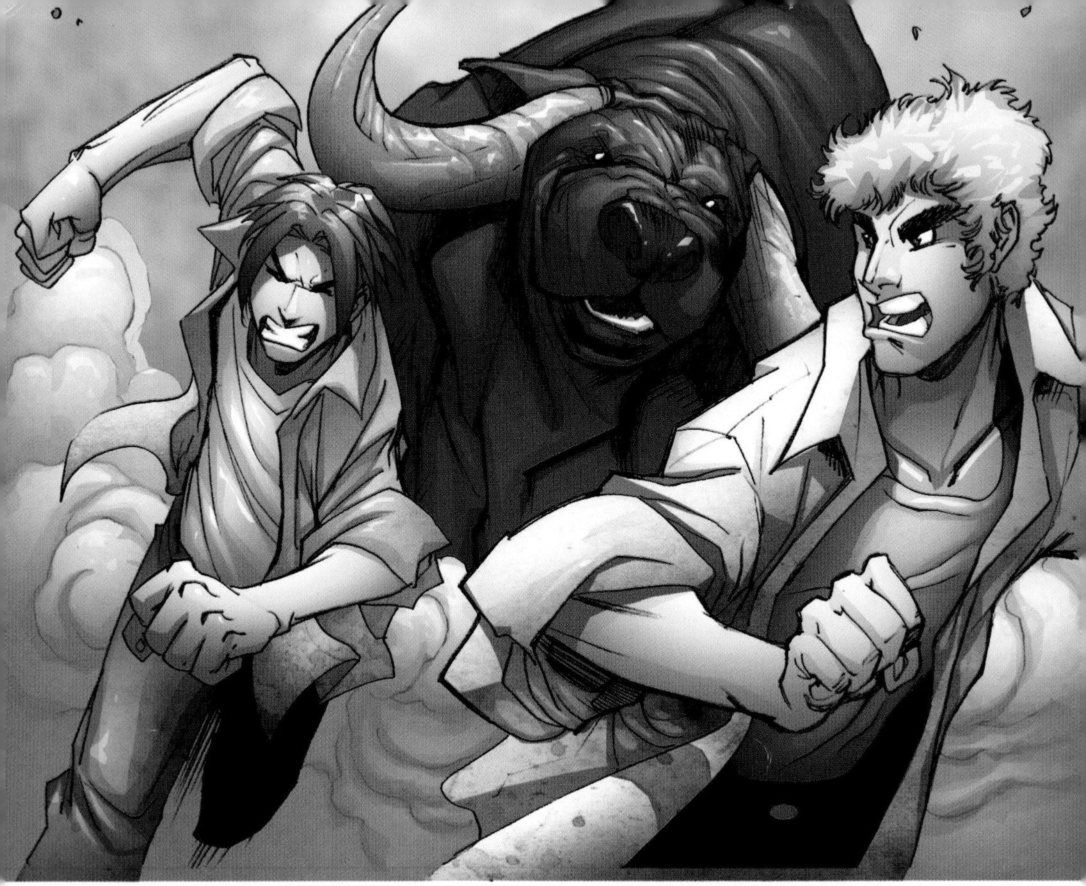

ABOUT THE RETELLING AUTHOR AND ILLUSTRATOR

Since 1986, author **Martin Powell** has been a freelance writer. He has written hundreds of stories, many of which have been published by Disney, Marvel, Tekno Comix, Moonstone Books, and others. In 1989, Powell received an Eisner Award nomination for his graphic novel *Scarlet in Gaslight*. This award is one of the highest comic book honors.

Gerardo Sandoval is a professional comic book illustrator from Mexico. He has worked on many well-known comics including Tomb Raider books from Top Cow Production. He has also worked on designs for posters and card sets.

GLOSSARY

albatross (AL-buh-tross)—a large seabird with webbed feet and long wings that can fly for a long time

horizon (huh-RYE-zuhn)—the line where the sky and the earth or sea seem to meet

looms (LOOMZ)—appears in a sudden or frightening way

magnificent (mag-NIF-i-sent)—very impressive or beautiful

mangroves (MANG-grohvz)—tropical trees

miracles (MEER-uh-kuhlz)—amazing events

New Guinea (NOO GIN-ee)—a large island north of Australia that is now called Papua New Guinea

peninsula (puh-NIN-suh-luh)—a piece of land surrounded by water on three sides that sticks out from a larger piece of land

prowling (PROUL-ing)—moving around quietly and secretly. A prowler is someone who is prowling.

savage (SAV-ij)—fierce, dangerous, wild

vanished (VAN-ishd)—disappeared suddenly

COMMON CORE ALIGNED
READING QUESTIONS

1. How does the Robinson family end up on a deserted island? What kinds of things do they encounter there? *("Refer to details and examples in a text when explaining what the text says.")*

2. The Robinsons have four children, and each child has his own unique personality. How can you tell each brother apart? *("Describe in depth a character, setting, or event in a story.")*

3. Ingenuity is the ability to come up with clever ideas to solve problems. Ingenuity is a significant theme in this graphic novel because all six of the Robinson family members demonstrate ingenuity. Find one example of ingenuity for each family member. *("Determine a theme of a story.")*

4. Juno and Turk are the Robinson family's dogs. What roles do the dogs play in this story? Find a few examples in the art and text of this book to support your answer. *("Describe in depth a character . . . drawing on specific details in the text.")*

5. While on the island, the family encounters both friendly and unfriendly plants and animals. Find two examples of each. *("Refer to details and examples in a text when explaining what the text says explicitly and when drawing inferences from the text.")*

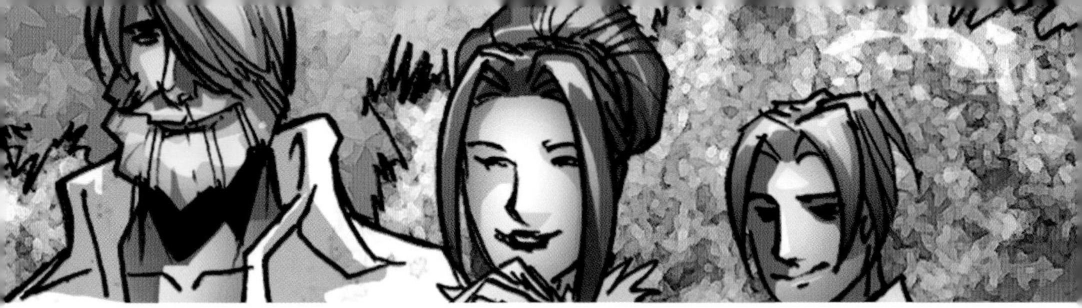

COMMON CORE ALIGNED
WRITING QUESTIONS

1. **Identify three situations from this story where exciting events happen. For each event, explain in your own words what happened, indicating page numbers where art or text supports your explanation.** *("Draw evidence from literary . . . texts to support analysis.")*

2. **If you and your family became stranded on a deserted island, what would you do in order to help you and your family survive? Would you make the same decisions as the Robinson family, or different ones? Why?** *("Write opinion pieces on topics or texts, supporting a point of view with reasons and information.")*

3. **While stranded on a deserted island, you find an old cell phone. You turn it on, and it works — but it only has enough power left to send a single text message. Who would you send a message to, and what exactly would it say?** *("Write informative/explanatory texts to examine a topic and convey ideas.")*

4. **Take the perspective of Juno the dog. If Juno could talk, what would it to say to the Robinson family? What might be the most important things to tell them?** *("Write narratives to develop real or imagined experiences or events.")*

5. **Take a close look at the illustrations in this graphic novel, focusing on the setting and scenery of the island. On a piece of paper, write a vivid and colorful description of the island based on details you see in the art.** *("Draw evidence from literary . . . texts to support analysis.")*

READ THEM ALL!

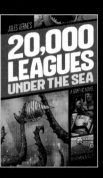

JULES VERNE'S
20,000 LEAGUES UNDER THE SEA
A GRAPHIC NOVEL
MARK TWAIN'S
THE ADVENTURES OF TOM SAWYER
A GRAPHIC NOVEL
ANNA SEWELL'S
BLACK BEAUTY
A GRAPHIC NOVEL
VICTOR HUGO'S
THE HUNCHBACK OF NOTRE DAME
A GRAPHIC NOVEL
ROBIN HOOD
A GRAPHIC NOVEL
ROBERT LOUIS STEVENSON'S
TREASURE ISLAND
A GRAPHIC NOVEL
MARY SHELLEY'S
FRANKENSTEIN
A GRAPHIC NOVEL
JULES VERNE'S
JOURNEY TO THE CENTER OF THE EARTH
A GRAPHIC NOVEL
ROBERT LOUIS STEVENSON'S
THE STRANGE CASE OF DR. JEKYLL AND MR. HYDE
A GRAPHIC NOVEL
BY BOWEN & FERRAN
WASHINGTON IRVING'S
THE LEGEND OF SLEEPY HOLLOW
A GRAPHIC NOVEL
DRACULA
JONATHAN SWIFT'S
GULLIVER'S TRAVELS
A GRAPHIC NOVEL
ARTHUR CONAN DOYLE'S
THE HOUND OF THE BASKERVILLES
A GRAPHIC NOVEL

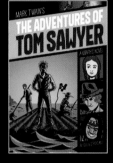

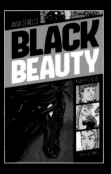

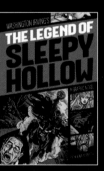

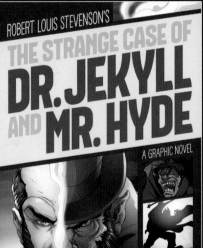

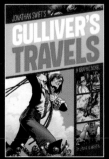

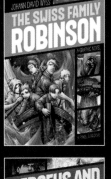

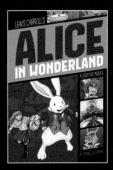
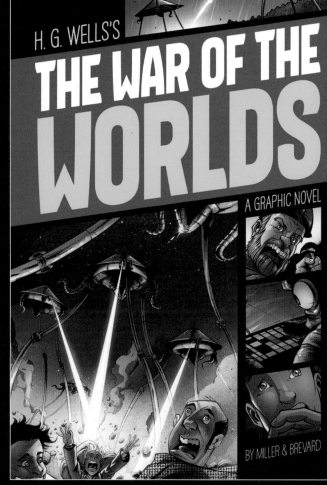

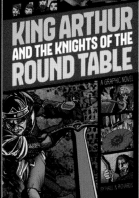
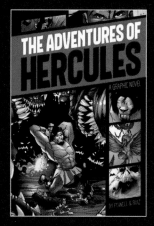